# REWRITE THE DEAD

## JON SMITH

BAL
KON
media

REWRITE THE DEAD
Published by Balkon Media

Paperback edition ISBN: 978-1-916970-20-5
Also available as an E-book



A CIP catalogue record for this title is available from the British Library.

Cover Illustrations & Design: Balkon Media

# ALSO BY JON SMITH

## FICTION

The Fifth Horseman

Destiny Can Bite Me (Fang & Loathing #1)

The Stakeout Diaries (Fang & Loathing #2)

Rewrite the Dead (Fang & Loathing #3)

## YOUNG ADULT

The Arb

## CHILDREN'S FICTION

Toytopia

## NON-FICTION

Once Upon A Brand

Founder Mode

The Bloke's Guide To Pregnancy

The Bloke's Guide To Babies

Get Into Bed With Google

Google Adwords That Work

Smarter Business Start-Ups

Start An Online Business

Digital Marketing For Businesses

# ONE

The Court of Pale Affairs' courtyard only came alive at dusk, which was precisely why it felt so dead inside. Vincent loitered just inside the archway, smoking a borrowed cigarette and listening to the chorus of well-manicured footsteps echoing off cold flagstones. An audience of vampires—some vintage, some nouveau—dotted the procession in a careful arrangement that spoke less of community and more of crowd control. Someone had even dusted the banisters.

He eyed the ceremonial duel circle at the centre of the flagstones, its boundary picked out in white chalk and iron posts hammered at regular intervals, each one festooned with more wards than a paranoid bookie's front door. Even the blood splatters from last month's "leadership training event" had been buffed away, leaving only faint reddish ghosts in the grain.

Ren trotted up beside him, messenger bag slung so low it threatened to trip her. "Is it me, or do they have more security than last time?" She nodded towards the perimeter, where a dozen glamoured mortals in matching yellow security polos played at nonchalance.

"Nothing says 'we're just a friendly historical society' like ringfencing your ancient magical duel with a bunch of ex-boxers from Lewisham," Vincent murmured. "If one of them so much as taps me with a metal detector, I'm filing a complaint."

Ren checked her phone, then arched an eyebrow. "You don't even have an email address."

Vincent exhaled smoke and smirked. "I'll set one up just to tell them to sod off. Assuming we live that long."

Mrs Barley arrived in full Housekeeper Mode, pin-straight, hair fixed, her only ornament a cluster of polished buttons that probably doubled as anti-possession charms. Next to her, Zara hovered a few inches above the cobblestone floor. Vincent caught her assessing the duel circle, lips twitching in private calculation.

"Excellent, you're all here," said Mrs Barley, steering them toward the velvet rope cordoning off the inner circle. "Let's try not to attract undue attention."

"Bit late for that," muttered Ren, glancing at the stewards collecting blood signatures and glamour chits at the entrance. She palmed a plastic card from her bag and slid it to the security golem with only minimal hissing.

Inside the rope, the elite had gathered: dozens of the Pale Affairs Council's finest in various states of decomposition, plus their mortal pets, hangers-on, and the odd Moderniser hoping to livestream vampire drama to their "Unfiltered Gothic" channel. At least two reality show runners clustered near the back, angling for a clear shot of the circle with cameras disguised as water bottles.

At the centre, already mid-oration, stood Elder Mortimer Blackthorn, Chair of the London Council and living proof that nepotism could in fact last forever. He was built like a disused hatstand—long, skeletal, draped in ceremonial robes that must have been hideous even when they were in style. His hair shone like an oil spill under the lanterns, and his eyebrows had gone rogue decades ago.

He held court from the raised platform, voice pitched to the farthest column. "—and so, by the sacred compact of the Keepers' Conclave, we reaffirm our commitment to dignity, discretion, and—above all—continuity in the face of destabilising elements. Let tonight be an example of our resolve."

A ripple of applause went up, more polite than sincere.

Vincent leaned in to Ren. "Nothing says continuity like fighting to the death in a chalk circle."

She elbowed him. "Shush. You promised not to get us evicted until after someone bleeds."

"Technically I said, 'after the first round.' Details matter."

Zara, not bothering to hide her yawn, murmured, "If he says 'historic moment' again, I will set myself on fire. You're all invited."

Mrs Barley flicked her a look. "Resist the impulse, dear. There's enough smoke in the air already."

Blackthorn's speech meandered through the standard platitudes: vampires as stewards of civilisation, the Council's ancient legacy, the importance of keeping up appearances for the benefit of "our less fortunate, sunlit kin." Vincent tuned out, watching instead the minor dramas in the crowd—a junior vampire stifling giggles at her elder's cravat, a Moderniser gleefully subtitling the speech in real-time ("#RespectTheDrip"), a couple of visiting Berliners snorting something phosphorescent off a business card.

The air changed when the side doors banged open, brass handles scraping against stone. The entire assembly turned as one, a Mexican wave of predatory attention. Vincent felt the hairs on his arms prickle.

Lord Ashcroft entered like he owned the concept of drama. Tall, waxen, dressed in Victorian mourning black with a frock coat that trailed dust. His face was the poster child for "haunted," sharp and spectral and lit from within by a hunger that made the entire space colder. He moved with a swagger both stylish and slightly off-kilter, as if each limb was being remotely piloted by pure contempt.

Vincent nearly choked on his cigarette. "Oh, hell. That's Ashcroft."

Ren's mouth dropped open. "The Ashcroft? The one from the duelling scandals?"

Mrs Barley's hands fluttered, ever so briefly, at her sides. "He's not supposed to be here," she whispered. "Not after Vienna."

Zara's eyebrows hit her hairline. "The Council's letting him duel? Do they want a massacre?"

Blackthorn, visibly unsettled, tried to continue his speech, but Ashcroft was already gliding toward the platform, cutting through the crowd like a frostbitten knife. He mounted the steps, bowing once, mockingly, to the Elder.

"My apologies, Council," Ashcroft announced, voice crisp and hollow, "but I believe I am owed the right to speak under the ancient law of invocation. Or has the Chair forgotten his own lineage?"

A sharp murmur, followed by a distinct shuffle of feet from the security golems. Blackthorn's grip tightened on the lectern.

"You are most certainly not owed the floor, Lord Ashcroft," Blackthorn hissed, "and you will address this Council with the decorum—"

Ashcroft grinned, revealing fangs so pristine they must have come with a warranty. "Decorum is for those who still possess a heart. Or a Council worth serving." He pivoted to the assembled crowd, his voice rising. "What say you, my fellow damned? Would you see your fate dictated by clerks and ledger men? Or will you stand as the architects of your own ending?"

Several dozen voices, half of them already drunk, shouted approval. Phones and enchanted recorders tilted upward in anticipation. Vincent felt the temperature of the courtyard drop another few degrees.

Ren whispered, "He's working the crowd. Old trick."

Vincent nodded. "Worked in Paris. Worked in Moscow. Every time he does this, something explodes."

Ashcroft faced Blackthorn, all traces of irony stripped from his voice. "By right of invocation and by the blood of my line, I challenge the Elder to single combat. May the Council bear witness."

A heavy silence, broken only by the faint click of a hundred phones recording history and the distant sound of someone fainting in the influencer section.

Blackthorn flushed—impressive, considering his pallor. "You are a disgrace to this Council. This is not the century for theatrical violence. Our affairs must remain secret, and you threaten—"

"Secrecy?" Ashcroft's laugh was thin and bitter. "You can't

even keep your own house in order. The Modernisers run amok, the humans are onto us, and you propose... paperwork." He spat the last word. "Let's do it properly. Like in the old days. Unless you're afraid."

Blackthorn bristled. He straightened to his full, intimidating height, which was at least an inch less than Ashcroft's. "I accept your challenge. May your idiocy be brief."

Ashcroft bowed, then raised his arms to the crowd. The ritual invocation shimmered around the circle—a translucent band of violet, ink-like light that snapped into place with a sound like glass breaking. The magical contract settled over the courtyard, pressing against Vincent's skin with an unpleasant, clammy insistence. No one, not even the Council's most jaded, could leave or intervene until the duel concluded.

Vincent turned to Mrs Barley. "Tell me you have a plan for this."

She pressed her lips together. "We survive. And if possible, we ensure there's something left to inherit."

Vincent watched the circle, the wards flaring with anticipation, and wondered if there was a way to bluff the universe's most self-important bureaucracy. He rather doubted it.

The crowd vibrated with excitement, the scent of ancient bloodlust and anticipation filling the air. The influencers jostled for position; the Berliners started a betting pool on who would bleed first; even the rent-a-cops leaned in, hoping to see some live-action vampire carnage. Ashcroft stood at the edge of the circle, already basking in the attention, while Blackthorn made a show of adjusting his ceremonial sash.

"Well," said Vincent, stubbing out his cigarette and dusting chalk from his shoes. "That's one way to open a meeting."

Ren grinned, dark eyes flickering with thrill. "Only in London."

Blackthorn shed his robes for the occasion, revealing the sleek, death's-head form of a vampire who had never, in his five centuries, faced meaningful exercise. His gloves were kid leather and gleamed, as did the ceremonial sabre strapped to his side—a relic so ancient Vincent suspected it might have never been used in combat.

Ashcroft, meanwhile, had no intention of playing to the rules. He flicked off his frock coat, planted his feet wide, and produced from the depths of his jacket a walking stick capped with a gleaming silver knob. He twirled it once, then stabbed the butt into the ground, the tip sparking against the stone.

"Brilliant," Vincent muttered, arms crossed. "Two antiques smashing each other to bits over who gets to sit at the posh end of the table. I've missed Eastenders for this."

Mrs Barley's grip closed on his biceps, surprisingly forceful for a woman who could iron shirts with the power of a disappointed frown. "Pay attention," she said. "Once invoked, the duel cannot be stopped. Not by Council, not by law, not by anyone."

Vincent snorted. "What about common sense?"

Mrs Barley's lips thinned. "That's always optional."

The duel circle shimmered, sigils along the iron fence posts lighting up in sequence—a macabre runway show. Blackthorn raised his sabre with a theatrical flourish and, with a muttered

Latin phrase, released a stream of after-images—half a dozen blurry doubles, all equally self-satisfied.

The crowd oohed, as much as a vampire crowd ever oohed. Some even clapped. Several mortals angled their phones to get a shot of the effect, filters at the ready.

Ashcroft didn't wait for applause. He lunged, closing the distance in a blink. His cane caught one of the after-images—a glittering spray of ink and illusion—and continued straight through to the original Blackthorn, slamming into his ribcage with a dull, wet crack.

"Nice party trick," Ashcroft sneered, cane swinging in brutal arcs. "Did you learn that at public school, or were you always this tedious?"

Blackthorn staggered, rallied, then struck with the sabre—an elegant, arcing swipe. Ashcroft dropped low, letting the blade sing over his scalp, and jabbed the cane up under Blackthorn's chin. There was a pop, a noise like an old lightbulb blowing, and for a moment every sigil around the circle flickered.

Vincent watched, fascinated, as Blackthorn reeled, his carefully constructed glamour breaking down. The ancient Elder looked up, teeth bared, but his doubles flickered and died. The courtyard was silent except for Ashcroft's shallow, delighted breathing.

"Why's no one stopping this?" Ren whispered, eyes wide.

Mrs Barley didn't let go of Vincent's arm. "Because the alternative is chaos. And vampires are nothing if not terrified of chaos."

"Sure, looks like chaos to me."

"You haven't seen chaos yet, dear."

Ashcroft circled, cane held out like a fencing foil. "You

never learned, did you, Morty? Always hiding behind rules and paperwork. Always afraid of the real blood." His tongue flicked over a fang; his eyes flashed. "Let's show them."

He came in with a fury that seemed to tear the air itself—blurring, reappearing, every motion exaggerated by the glamour radiating off the duel circle. Blackthorn blocked the first blow, the second, but the third took him in the leg, sending him sprawling. Ashcroft pounced, driving the Elder back against the iron posts.

With a flourish, he caught Blackthorn's throat in the crook of his cane, levered him upwards, and twisted. There was a crunch that echoed through the courtyard.

Blackthorn dangled, feet scrabbling, cape flapping like a dislocated bat. He tried to summon another glamour, but Ashcroft simply leaned in, and bit.

Not a genteel, cinema-vampire bite, but a full predatory mauling, fangs going for the jugular with a violence that made even the Modernisers lower their phones in shock.

Vincent felt the urge to move, to interfere, but Mrs Barley held him firm. "Duelling law. Break it, and you're next," she hissed.

He glanced sideways and found even Zara, usually unflappable, looking vaguely ill. "I thought these things were supposed to end with an apology and a handshake," Vincent murmured.

"Not this century," Zara replied. "Not for Ashcroft."

The duel ended as abruptly as it began: Blackthorn slumped to the flagstones, blood pouring in ugly black rivulets down the front of his cravat. Ashcroft wiped his mouth with a lace handkerchief, then turned to the assembled Council with a bow so deep it bordered on parody.

"Ladies and gentlemen of the Council," he announced, voice ringing clear, "the Draft Eternal has written your ending." He snapped his fingers, and a pulse of magic shot up the iron posts, sending a ripple through every vampire in attendance.

In the silence, Ashcroft stepped down from the circle, frock coat immaculate, not a speck of blood on his lips. He walked the perimeter, soaking in the panic.

The crowd surged and stuttered, unsure whether to run or applaud. Some filmed; some fainted. The Modernisers, showing admirable professionalism, resumed livestreaming with breathless commentary.

Ren exhaled, only now realising she'd been holding her breath. "Are we safe?"

Vincent watched Ashcroft preen before the horror-struck masses. "Define safe."

Ashcroft turned at that precise moment, as if he'd heard. His gaze found Vincent, lingered, and smiled. "Exquisite, isn't it? So much history to be rewritten. Perhaps you'll play your part better this time, Vincent Lupo."

He winked.

Vincent scowled. "Next time I ghostwrite someone's legacy, remind me to demand hazard pay."

Mrs Barley patted his shoulder. "Let's go. There'll be fall-out, and we need to plan."

As the Council dissolved into chaos—security golems chasing feral vampires, mortals shrieking and posting in real time—Vincent led his crew through the back corridors, the sound of duelling law and supernatural contract fading behind them.

# TWO

The Council's private chamber had once been an abbey refectory, its vaults carved to direct choir song up towards a God who'd stopped taking their calls centuries ago. Now the vaulting served mainly to concentrate bureaucratic panic into a sort of operatic feedback loop. Beneath it, the Council elders fanned out around a horseshoe of walnut desks, raising their voices with all the decorum of a family court just after the judge walked out.

Iron chandeliers swung overhead, scattering warped shadows onto the desks below—each desk still humming, faintly, with the residual magic of the duel circle. Some elders had left off their wigs in the confusion; others clung to old-world dignity, powder caked on like embalming paste.

Vincent slouched at the periphery, shoulders wedged against the cold stone, arms folded and jaw set. A cigarette balanced in an ornate silver holder, the sort of thing that suggested both class and terminal boredom. He watched the debate as one might observe a dog show where the dogs had eaten their handlers.

Ren had snagged a battered chair and perched on its back legs, feet on the seat, all the better to scan the room for improvised exits. She caught Vincent's eye and waggled her eyebrows, which could have meant "this is all bollocks" or "we could definitely rob these people blind before sunrise." Vincent, who'd worked with her long enough to know it was both, allowed himself the ghost of a grin.

Mrs Barley stood a discreet two metres away, clipboard in hand and expression of gentle exasperation nailed to her face. She flicked her gaze from desk to desk, taking notes on every outburst, as if planning to file an incident report with God Himself. The polished buttons on her lapel glinted whenever she moved; they looked like nothing, but Vincent would have bet his next month's rent that one was an active panic button.

Overhead, Zara's ghost drifted through a rib of vaulting, arms crossed, hair immaculate as always despite the lack of gravitational fidelity. "Nothing inspires unity like abject panic," she observed, projecting her voice just enough to make the nearest elder glance around uneasily.

"They're not panicking," Mrs Barley replied, sotto voce. "They're simply expressing a diversity of opinions under duress."

Zara made a rude gesture only Ren could appreciate.

Below, the Council had resolved itself into a tripartite argument, represented by three Elders whose faces alone could have won a Halloween costume contest.

Elder Corvane, a spindly thing in a pinstripe that screamed "mortgage fraud," stabbed the desk with a finger. "We must act decisively. Retaliate at once. Otherwise, what's the point of a Council?"

Elder Skye, who wore a spiderweb of steel jewellery over a velvet suit, retorted, "Yes, let's 'retaliate' against a myth. Very sensible. Are you also afraid of the bogeyman, Corvane, or just losing your pension?"

At the centre, Elder Marwood leaned forward, voice pitched for maximum gravitas. "All we know is this: Lord Ashcroft has invoked the Draft Eternal. This is not conjecture. This is not a prank. The old duelling law locked us all into that circle. He bound the Council's collective will and now—" he gestured out to the courtyard from whence Blackthorn was despatched, "—he owns it."

A general susurrus. Several elders muttered about memory suppression spells. One suggested calling in the Modernisers, if only so they could be blamed later.

Vincent picked a fleck of tobacco from his tongue and let the room's tension ferment. In the best-case scenario, the elders would tear each other apart and he could nick the good cutlery on the way out. Worst case, they would remember the standing tradition: When in existential peril, draft Vincent Lupo.

Ren leaned over, whispering, "Odds on who gets bricked first?"

Vincent considered. "Marwood's got the voice, but Corvane's got a real talent for being shanked in alleys. Even odds."

Zara drifted lower, face passing straight through a hanging lantern. "Are you going to tell them, or shall I?"

He shrugged. "They'll get there. Vampires are nothing if not addicted to their own drama."

The Council's debate trended rapidly towards the unhinged. Marwood banged a gavel for order, but it had the acoustic impact of a polite knock on a tomb.

Corvane rose, skeletal hands spread as if presenting a corpse at a wake. "I move that we suppress all memory of this incident. Contain the narrative, and resume business as usual. We cannot afford chaos. The last time a prophecy ran viral, we lost Paris for a century."

Skye laughed, high and bright. "I'm sure the humans will be very understanding when their entire Parliament is shredded by historical cosplayers. Yes, let's just not mention it and maybe the apocalypse will go away."

Vincent flicked his cigarette butt into an empty chalice and cleared his throat. "If it helps, nobody outside this room takes the Draft Eternal seriously. You're all ahead of the PR curve."

A dozen eyes snapped to him in unison, like a murder of crows clocking a shiny bauble.

Corvane's lips peeled back, equal parts smile and snarl. "Do I know you?"

"Vincent Lupo. Professional liability. Unofficially on retainer for the Council, when you need deniable assets or a very poor memoir ghostwritten."

Skye stared. "Weren't you supposed to be dead?"

Vincent gave a noncommittal hand wobble. "Took a sabbatical. Got bored. Now I'm here."

Elder Marwood steepled his fingers, voice icy. "If you know something about the Draft Eternal, Mr Lupo, I suggest you share it."

Vincent waited, just long enough to annoy them. "Not much to share. Every vampire's heard the myth—a living prophecy, a narrative engine that rewrites history from the shadows. I thought it was just an excuse to burn old diaries."

Zara drifted to his shoulder, whispering, "You know it's real. You've seen it. Stop playing for time."

Vincent flicked his eyes up, subtle. "I've seen a lot of things. The myth goes: The Draft Eternal is a kind of self-editing story, a recursive loop in the fabric of vampire history. Every time someone tries to change the order of things, the Draft flexes, and someone—usually the loudest—gets deleted."

Corvane huffed. "So, we're being threatened by a recursive metaphor?"

"Not a metaphor," Marwood corrected. "An entity. One that can only be invoked under very specific circumstances— public duel, witnessed by a quorum, a challenge to the legitimacy of the Council." He gestured at the room. "Which, I believe, has just happened."

Ren shifted in her seat, voice low. "So... he's what, a vampire ghostwriter? Editing reality?"

Mrs Barley smiled thinly. "That would be poetic. But the Draft is less a writer, more a parasite. It adapts, learns, and erases what it can't control."

Vincent looked at the ceiling, trying to avoid thinking of Carmine. Of Paris. Of the last time he'd seen a prophecy turn viral and chew through a city block by block.

Marwood nodded at the bloodstain. "Ashcroft has a plan, and now he has the Council's signature. We must pre-empt him before the Draft sets the new story in stone."

"Good luck with that," Zara said, but only Vincent heard her.

The argument spiralled again—some demanding armed

intervention, others frantically compiling lists of plausible deni-ability. Someone suggested a full recall of the Modernisers; another elder floated the idea of hiring mortal consultants, which was met with a derisive snort and a whispered "They'd just unionise."

Through it all, Vincent stood, arms folded, cigarette holder bobbing as he gnawed on the tip. Every minute spent bickering was a minute closer to whatever Ashcroft was orchestrating. He tapped a finger against his sleeve, an old, nervous habit Carmine had once likened to "a metronome for impending doom."

It was Elder Corvane who finally cracked. He rounded on Vincent, voice gone sharp as frost. "You ended Carmine. You will end this."

The chamber fell into sudden, juddering quiet.

Vincent regarded Corvane with the look of a man who'd been volunteered for a suicide pact after missing the last three meetings. He let the silence ripen, then gave a bow so theatrical it bordered on the obscene.

"Ah, so I'm a hero now? What an upgrade from 'liability'." His smile was sharp, but his fingers drummed the edge of the desk like hail on a coffin lid.

Ren grinned. Mrs Barley made a note. Zara, for the first time, looked sympathetic.

Vincent straightened. "You want me to hunt Ashcroft? Or the Draft itself?"

Marwood's smile was all teeth. "You know the difference?"

Vincent shrugged, hands open. "Only one of them bleeds when you hit it."

The Council returned to its squabbling, the matter settled in the way only true bureaucracies can: by punting the existential football to whoever happened to be closest to the door. Vincent slouched back, cigarette holder between his teeth, and wondered if he'd ever met a prophecy that didn't end with someone being rewritten.

He doubted it. But there was a first time for everything.

The Council's situation room resembled a bomb shelter that had been hastily redecorated by an overzealous prepper with a fetish for leather-bound books. A half-moon table faced a wall of enchanted maps, the geography of London puckered and twitching as new disturbances pulsed to life. Magic clung to every surface: in the hairline fractures of the marble floor, in the ink that bled from ancient ledgers, in the faint ozone stink that suggested one too many reality adjustments.

Vincent stood with his back to the main door, hands in his pockets, as the Council's "crisis committee" rearranged itself for the briefing. Only the truly desperate called it a "briefing." To Vincent, it looked more like a last rites ceremony with bad PowerPoint.

A golem intern wheeled out a tray of blood vials and espresso shots. Ren grabbed a double and scowled at the projected map, already bored by the dots blooming across the river. Zara's ghost perched on the edge of the projection, swinging her legs through a Ley Line, tracing the pattern of mayhem with a finger.

Mrs Barley stood just behind Vincent, reading the room in her efficient way. She noted every tremor, every clench of a jaw, every sidelong glance to the growing stain on the agenda: Ashcroft, now highlighted in funereal black, with his "manifestations" swarming across the Thames like a plague of particularly ostentatious wasps.

Elder Skye started the show. "The entity calling itself Ashcroft—"

"Still Ashcroft," muttered Ren, who'd read the man's file. "He's got a real brand loyalty thing."

Skye ignored her. "—has not merely overthrown protocol, he's raised a hit parade of British infamy. In the last four hours, we've logged twelve high-value necromantic events. Each time, the same: a historical figure, deceased for at least a century, returns. Revenant, but smarter. Hungry for something other than blood."

A gesture, and the map spat out a new red pin. "Oxford Street, two hours ago. A Regency poisoner with a side interest in vivisection. Killed three, then attempted to petition for clemency with the Home Office."

Ren snorted. "Classic Londoner. Murder, then bureaucracy."

A ripple of nervous titters from the assembled. Even the Council's best and brightest couldn't quite believe the shape of the apocalypse they'd been handed.

Elder Corvane took over, flicking his tongue as if sampling the air for loose narratives. "The sightings are escalating. Every historical monster with a grievance is crawling out of the paper shredder. Some are gunning for us, others seem content to air old scores in public. Either way, we're losing containment."

Vincent studied the map, ignoring the press of eyes. It looked like someone had set up a game of plague chess and then spilled the pieces. "You think Ashcroft's controlling them directly?" he asked, more for Mrs Barley's benefit than the room.

Marwood, ever the peacemaker, interjected. "Not control, so much as orchestration. The Draft Eternal wants to overwrite reality; Ashcroft is just feeding it the right names at the right time. Each revenant weakens the boundary between stories. If he can flip enough points of history—"

Zara finished the thought, her voice faintly overlapping Marwood's in the way only dead people could manage: "—then we're not living in our history anymore. We're living in his edit."

Mrs Barley made a small, precise sound of distaste. "He's rebooting London as a theatre for his own script. Vampires included."

The map changed again. This time, the pins weren't red but a queasy shade of green. "Moderniser activity?" Vincent asked, recognising a cluster at King's Cross.

Skye grimaced. "They're treating it like a festival. New faces, new power structure, a chance to 'disrupt' the old order. Some of them are helping us, others are livestreaming the chaos. It's fracturing the city."

Corvane jabbed a knuckle at Vincent. "Which is why we need someone who can operate on both sides. The Modernisers don't trust us. The old guard don't trust anyone. But they all know you, Lupo."

Vincent looked unimpressed. "And your plan is what, exactly? Send me round to all the blood banks and tell everyone to play nice until the prophecy blows over?"

Skye laced her fingers together. "You have contacts in every coven, every clique. You're not a joiner, but you're a connector. We need you to build a coalition."

Ren nearly choked on her espresso. "You want him to be a recruiter?"

Mrs Barley's clipboard snapped shut with military efficiency. "They want him to unite the city. By any means. Traditionalists, Modernisers, the criminal elements. Anyone not yet co-opted by Ashcroft."

Vincent laughed, but it came out dry and splintery. "Me? Unite vampires? You've met me, right?"

Zara's ghost leant down, lips brushing his ear: "You're not as bad at this as you pretend."

He didn't dignify that with a response.

Corvane, stung by the insubordination, raised his voice. "This is not a request, Lupo. You are uniquely compromised—"

"Qualified," Marwood corrected, though his smile made it clear which word he'd have chosen.

Vincent rolled his eyes, but the performance was for the room. Under the surface, he could feel the low, leaden dread that always preceded disaster: the prickling sense that once again, he'd let himself be drawn into someone else's war.

Mrs Barley laid a gentle, iron-hard hand on his shoulder. "You don't have to do it alone. But you do have to do it."

Ren tilted her head, watching him with that unnerving stillness that always suggested she was two moves ahead. She'd been waiting for his jokes, but now she tracked the way his knuckles whitened on the chair back, the way he never quite unclenched his jaw.

"Fine," Vincent said at last, voice flat. "You want a coalition,

I'll build you one. But when this all goes to shit, don't pretend you didn't see it coming."

Marwood nodded. "Consider it seen."

The Council moved on to secondary concerns—damage control, glamour deployment, plausible deniability—but Vincent stopped listening. Instead, he mapped out the city in his head: the safe houses, the feeding dens, the old-world hangouts and the startup bars where the Modernisers gathered to sell each other on the new vampire capitalism. He tried to picture which faces would still be intact after a week of Ashcroft's rampage.

He did not like the answer.

Ren nudged his knee under the table, a signal to get moving. He followed, with Mrs Barley and Zara's ghost trailing behind.

As they walked the corridor—ancient, candlelit, filled with the echoes of a thousand political betrayals—Vincent let his guard slip for half a second. Shoulders dropped, and he exhaled a long, slow breath that steamed in the cold. "They want a saviour. All they've got is me."

Mrs Barley didn't look back, but she must have heard, because her lips twitched at the corners.

The iron doors swung shut behind them, their echo sealing the moment.

# THREE

They left the Court of Pale Affairs by the back door, which was the only one not crawling with legal aides, PR sorcerers, and whatever the collective noun was for vampires in committee. The passage let out onto a sloped street somewhere between Westminster and Purgatory, the city's sodium glare bleeding through ancient stained glass. Vincent paused at the threshold, lighting a cigarette mostly for the drama, and waited for the others to shuffle into step.

Ren emerged first, face set to "predator on the way to the job centre," hoodie up and hands in her pockets. Behind her, Mrs Barley conducted a brisk headcount, followed by a spectral Zara whose shoes made no sound but whose presence turned the alley at least five degrees colder.

Vincent gave the city a once-over, as if expecting it to have replaced itself with something better while he'd been indoors. London had not. It wore its night like a greasy trench coat, flashing the odd bare thigh of elegance but mostly stinking of old rain and low intent.

"Council's in meltdown," Ren observed, glancing back over her shoulder as if expecting the building to detonate out of sheer embarrassment. "You think they'll ever admit they have no idea what they're doing?"

"Only on their deathbed," Vincent said. "And even then, it'll be a subcommittee confession, redacted for public release."

Mrs Barley tutted, as if this were a breach of household protocol. "They'll muddle through, dear. They always do."

Zara floated beside them, arms folded, scanning the street as if she expected to see crime statistics manifest physically. "You realise that if Ashcroft gets another hour head start, he'll have a narrative lock on half the city?"

"Let him," Vincent said, flicking ash onto a centuries-old paving stone. "The old guard loves a comeback tour. Maybe he'll rebrand Parliament as a theme park."

They walked in silence for a moment, the sounds of late-night London filtering in: cabbies squabbling with Uber drivers, the squeal of a kebab shop window fight, two bin lorries negotiating the right of way like sumo wrestlers on benzos. Overhead, a neon sign blinked in binary, advertising "24hr Off-License & Blood Bank," the latter an in-joke for those with the right predilections.

They turned onto Whitehall, heading for the river. The tourist overflow had ebbed for the night, leaving only the hard-core insomniacs and the sort of people who believed four a.m. was the best time to propose on Westminster Bridge. The city looked empty, but Vincent could feel the air tense, as if London itself was bracing for a particularly nasty thunderstorm.

It was Ren who spotted the first anomaly. "Wasn't there a statue here last week?"

Vincent glanced at the familiar bronze of Sir Winston Churchill, arm stuffed into his greatcoat. "Still is. He's just grown a better suit."

But Ren was right. The face, once the chubby mask of twentieth-century authority, had changed. The cheekbones were sharper, the lips pursed in a smirk rather than a scowl, and the eyes—previously glassy with historical compromise—were now alive with a kind of predatory amusement.

Mrs Barley stepped forward, peering up with the professional interest of a woman who'd seen more than one mausoleum get the facelift treatment. "That's not the original face," she said. "I think that's—goodness, what was his name? The industrialist. Built the first railway into the City, then vanished after the stock crash."

Zara's ghost shimmered. "History's being rewritten. Ashcroft's not just summoning revenants—he's massaging the entire timeline."

Vincent arched an eyebrow. "And here I thought reality had hit rock bottom in the nineties."

They pressed on, growing more alert with every block. The city was doing its best to behave, but now that they'd noticed, the glitches were everywhere: blue plaques on buildings shifting names mid-sentence, the streetlights adjusting their hues to match the period mood, shopfronts morphing from 24-hour vape emporia to "Chymist & Co. – Leeching Services." Once, Vincent glanced back and saw Churchill's statue had turned its head to watch them pass, a trick even he had to admire.

By the time they reached the Embankment, the alterations were impossible to ignore. A row of benches, recently vandalised with "BREXIT WAS A FEVER DREAM," now bore instead the slogan "BRING BACK THE EMPIRE," in elegant serif script. A child's balloon, drifting above the street, morphed from Spider-Man to a delicately painted Punchinello as they watched.

Ren stopped dead, hand on the balustrade. "Does anyone else see the plaque on the bridge?"

Vincent squinted at the stonework. The dedication had gone from "Opened by Her Majesty Queen Elizabeth II, 1974," to "Baptised in the Blood of the Thames, Lord Ashcroft, 1867." Even the font was different: Gothic, baroque, bleeding into the mortar.

"I don't like this," Ren said. "It's like... the city's being live-tweeted by a Victorian goth."

Mrs Barley made a note of the date. "That was the year of the Bone Riots. London nearly tore itself apart."

"Still could," said Zara, voice faint and doubled. She hovered at the edge of the group, eyes flickering. "I feel the edit pushing. Like a draft trying to overwrite the living."

Vincent felt it too, now. The city's rhythm had gone arrhythmic, stuttering between centuries. Somewhere a few blocks over, a car alarm cut off mid-wail and was replaced by the clatter of horse-drawn carriages. Then both sounds layered, as if the city couldn't make up its mind whether it was today or 1887.

They turned onto a side street—a shortcut Ren insisted on, usually safe, usually full of cabbies and council grit. Tonight, it was empty. The paving stones changed under their feet, melting from cracked tarmac to perfect, rain-glossed cobbles. Gas lamps blinked into existence along the walk, burning with a cold, blue-white fire. The air changed: drier, tinged with coal dust, and alive with the echo of old footsteps.

Vincent reached out and touched a lamp post. It was solid, but it vibrated faintly, as if humming with suppressed energy.

Then the street flickered. For one second it was 1890, complete with raucous barrow boys and a street vendor hawking penny dreadfuls. Then it was now, the detritus of modernity—vomit, vape pens, discarded McMuffin wrappers—sprawled over the same flagstones. Then it snapped back, then forward, then both at once.

Ren yelped and staggered, clutching her left arm. "Ow. Fuck. It's hot."

Vincent saw the Mark on her forearm, glowing through the fabric like a neon wound. The lines were back, and now they pulsed, angry and alive, as if magnetised to every shift in the story.

"Is it getting worse?" he asked, keeping his voice light.

Ren shook her head, then nodded. "I don't know. It's like... every time the city edits, it's pulling at me."

Mrs Barley leaned in, inspecting the Mark with professional detachment. "The prophecy is trying to anchor itself to living witnesses," she mused. "If you resist, it will push harder."

"Great," Ren muttered. "Me again."

Zara hovered above them, hair stirring as if in a wind they couldn't feel. "The Draft Eternal isn't just rewriting history. It's looking for ways to make it stick. The more people who remember the new story, the more real it gets."

"Which means if enough of the city believes Ashcroft has always been here..." Vincent let the logic finish itself.

"...then he always has been," said Mrs Barley.

The street spasmed again. A shadow at the far end stretched and multiplied, resolving into the figure of a man in top hat and cloak. He paused, doffed the hat with a bow, then faded into the wall as the street snapped back to the twenty-first century. A bus thundered past, briefly breaking the illusion, but even the headlights seemed to smear into sepia as the edits fought for dominance.

They retreated to the main road, Vincent keeping Ren between himself and the traffic, just in case the Mark went nuclear. The city felt less like a place now and more like a stage, the scenery creaking under the strain of too many scriptwriters.

He turned to Mrs Barley, who hadn't stopped cataloguing the anomalies since the bridge. "How long until the edit's permanent?"

She pursed her lips. "Depends on the strength of the narrative. Right now, it's unstable, but if Ashcroft manages to bind the story to enough living minds—especially those with a stake in the outcome—it could lock in hours. Days, at best."

Zara said nothing, just drifted above them, eyes darting from shadow to shadow. Her outline blurred at the edges, as if the draft's revisions threatened to erase even the dead.

They paused at a corner, the city's lights flickering with uncanny intent. Vincent looked up, studying the skyline. A new structure had appeared, halfway built: a gothic spire of glass and iron, rising like a hangnail from the wrist of the Thames. He didn't remember it from before. He doubted anyone else did, either.

"It's a proof of concept," Vincent muttered. "The Draft Eternal's treating London like a manuscript in need of a proper editor."

Ren shivered, though the night wasn't cold. "I hate to break it to him, but his edits are shite."

Mrs Barley smiled, just a little. "They always are, dear. But that doesn't mean he won't get them published."

Vincent flicked his spent cigarette into the gutter, watching it vanish into a temporal crevasse. For the first time that night, his hands shook.

"We need a new plan," he said.

"Got one?" asked Ren.

"Not yet," Vincent replied, voice steadying. "But I know a few editors worse than death. And one of them owes me a favour."

Mrs Barley checked her notes. "Shall we regroup at Ren's?"

Zara gave a thumbs up, her hand blurring as if caught between two exposures.

Vincent nodded. "Lead the way, ghost of prophecies past."

And together, they threaded through the rewiring city, keeping to the bright places, careful not to look too long at anything that might look back.

They filed into the flat, and for a moment the chaos of central London was replaced by a different, denser sort of entropy. The place looked like a lending library had thrown up after a three-day bender. Books coated every surface: codices on the counter, monographs propping up the telly, a thigh-high drift of pamphlets covering the radiator. The air was thick with ozone and the subtle, corrosive tang of leaking ink.

"Wow," Vincent said to Ren. "You've been a busy bee."

"It's not me." Ren put up her hands in surrender. "Zara's been bulking on her research diet. I've just been watching telly mainly."

Zara's ghost hovered above her own sofa, feet tucked under her in the pose of someone who had spent too long working from home. She flicked her gaze at the mess. "Make yourselves at home, but don't touch anything with a date before 1939. Those ones are, um... active."

Vincent selected a seat with minimal paper shrapnel, making room for Ren, who immediately curled up cross-legged and started scrolling her phone. The Mark was still visible beneath her skin, now duller but pulsing in time with some private, sinister metronome.

Mrs Barley performed a fastidious sweep of the room, wiping at non-existent dust and then extracting a notepad from her jacket pocket. "You said you had a lead on Ashcroft," she prompted.

Zara nodded, gesturing to a pile of parchment so old it might have fossilised on contact with sunlight. "I pulled everything I could get hold off. But the interesting bits aren't what's there, it's what's missing. Whole lineages—erased. You look for them, it's like they never existed."

Vincent raised an eyebrow. "So, Ashcroft's not just returning. He's rewriting the prequel?"

Zara plucked a page from mid-air and held it up. It wept ink from its edges, like it was sweating out the effort of staying real.

"He's more than that. He's a relay. The Draft Eternal isn't a person, it's a… narrative parasite. A sentient editorial process. It latches onto unstable stories and uses them to propagate itself. Like with Carmine, but *cleverer*. Think of Ashcroft as the hand puppet, but the real bastard's the arm up his arse."

Ren snorted. "So, we're fighting a demon editor. Figures."

Mrs Barley read over Zara's shoulder, lips pursed. "And what's its objective, exactly? Beyond chaos for its own sake?"

"It's not chaos," Zara replied, voice sharp. "It's closure. Prophecies are supposed to die with their authors. But this one —Carmine's—never got a proper ending. The Draft Eternal's goal is to edit every anomaly out of existence. Including us."

A heavy, greasy silence settled on the room. Vincent felt it in his teeth, a pressure not unlike the first moments before a migraine. He tried to break the mood. "Good news is, I've been deleted from better stories than this. Bad news, this one's got sequels."

Nobody laughed, which seemed about right.

Mrs Barley began sorting the documents into crisp, symmetrical piles, occasionally straightening a corner with the kind of frown that could sand wood. "We need to locate Ashcroft before the Draft reaches critical mass. Once the narrative's established, you can't undo it without risking the whole city."

Ren's thumb hovered over her screen, but she was watching Vincent. "What about the Mark?" she asked. "It's not just reacting, it's… I don't know. Updating."

Zara drifted closer, peering at Ren's arm. Her ghostly hand passed through the flesh, but the Mark glowed brighter at the contact, casting fractal shadows on the wall. "It's a tracking device, and also a warning. The prophecy still recognises you as a narrative hazard. That's good. Means you're still unpredictable."

Ren's eyes narrowed. "Is this supposed to be comforting?"

"Not in the slightest," Zara deadpanned. "But you're alive, which in editorial terms is a running plot error."

Vincent watched all this, chewing the inside of his cheek. He felt the familiar urge to bolt—to vanish into some less-cursed version of London and leave the apocalypse to people who took it personally. As far as he was concerned he'd done his bit already by defeating Bartholemew and Carmine. But then he saw Mrs Barley, lining up the ink-bloody pages, and Ren, who'd stopped scrolling and was now flexing her arm as if she could force the Mark to behave through sheer stubbornness.

He realised, with an almost physical sense of defeat, that he was going to see this through.

Mrs Barley broke the silence. "Our enemy isn't just a vampire. It's an editor."

"Worse," Zara replied, her outline warping as she laughed. "It's the draft every editor throws away. The one that refuses to stay dead."

A tap at the window made them all jump. Vincent spun, but it was only a bundle of ravens settling on the sill, their eyes glittering. They watched through the glass, rapt, as if waiting for the scene to resolve itself.

Ren spoke, voice small but certain. "And I'm still part of the document."

Vincent tried a grin, but his fangs ached in his gums, and when he ran his tongue over them he tasted copper and regret. "Can we really fight this?"

Mrs Barley looked up, meeting his eyes. For the first time, her composure slipped. "We'll have to get creative."

Zara nodded. "I'll draft a plan." She grinned, ghostly and unsettling. "With edits."

Vincent raised his glass to the team, and this time, even the ravens seemed to approve.

# FOUR

Vincent hated the East End after dark, which was awkward for a creature who, by medical consensus, shouldn't have existed outside a windowless office suite. The streets were designed to resist navigation, having been laid out by the world's most vengeful cartographer, and after what the Blitz didn't flatten, gentrification had done its best to render unrecognisable. But even with the rerouted night buses, the pavement puke, and the running commentary from every passing minicab, the old ghosts still clung to the place.

Tonight, Vincent was in pursuit of a new ghost. The sort with a flair for the theatrical and a distressing disregard for property values.

The rumour had started as a text from a Council intern who'd once tried to blackmail him: "Check Curtain's Call, Brick Lane. Top floor. Unmissable." The fact that the informant was now a fine mist under the Charing Cross underpass didn't dampen the urgency. By the time Vincent, Ren, Mrs Barley, and the still-corporeally-challenged Zara reached the address, the street was already vibrating with the sort of anticipation that usually preceded either a riot or a pop-up mezcal bar.

Curtain's Call had been a theatre, once. The sign above the doorway was pitted, the "i" long since excised by generations of knife-wielding critics. The foyer reeked of brine and cheap incense, and the carpets underfoot gave up little clouds of spores with each step. Past the long-dead box office, through a maze of blackout curtains (none of which matched), they found the main house.

The auditorium was a mortuary diorama, perfect for the night's theme. Rows of velvet seats slumped in surrender, fabric scarred by cigarette burns and the occasional feral cat. The ceiling's chandelier—a monstrous thing, half-glass, half stalactite—hung so low that even Vincent had to duck beneath it. The footlights had been replaced with tea candles and, inexplicably, a handful of LED torches duct-taped to vodka bottles.

On stage: the world's most baroque punchline. Three coffins stood upright, painted in a gloss lacquer, arranged like contestants in a depraved beauty pageant. In front of them, Lord Ashcroft paced, arms spread, coat tails flapping like the wings of a murdered crow.

The audience was a curated fever dream. Mortals made up half—faces shining with the peculiar enthusiasm of cultists or extremely dedicated bloggers. The other half was vampires, the Moderniser set, phones at the ready, eager for a meme-worthy disaster. At least two had matching "BITE ME HARDER" t-shirts, and one wore a novelty top hat with "#GothDaddy" in rhinestones. Vincent felt a powerful urge to set them all on fire.

They took seats near the aisle, well within escape range but close enough to see the sweat on Ashcroft's brow. Or what passed for sweat on a man who, strictly speaking, lacked functioning glands.

Ashcroft waited for the murmurs to die down, then swept a hand in greeting. "Ladies, gentlemen, the ambiguously living!" he boomed, his voice slicing through the room's damp like a police siren on Bonfire Night. "Welcome to the first—of many—demonstrations. Tonight, we restore to London the lost legends it so desperately craves!"

Vincent muttered, "Nothing says 'legend' like an East End soft launch."

Ren snickered behind her hand. "I give it two acts before they eat the audience."

Mrs Barley scanned the crowd, taking inventory of faces and potential escape routes. "That would be an improvement," she said, adjusting her glasses. "At least then they'd be occupied."

Zara hovered a seat's width above her cushion, eyes locked on the stage. "Watch his hands," she whispered. "He's binding the crowd. Literally."

Ashcroft approached the first coffin. With a theatrical flourish, he unlatched the brass clasps and stepped aside as the lid creaked open.

The occupant emerged with exquisite slowness, as if unwilling to disturb her own narrative tension. She wore a gown of iridescent black feathers, face painted with the delicate precision of a master forger. Her lips, glossy and cyanotic, parted in a smile so sharp it might have been carved with a palette knife.

"Allow me to introduce," said Ashcroft, "the jewel of Mayfair, the original arsenic angel: Lady Euphemia Clore!"

The audience roared, phones flashing, as the revenant socialite glided forward. Her hands, encased in elbow-length gloves, fluttered a jewelled fan with wrist-breaking elegance. The fan's tips, Vincent noted, dripped with a fluid that steamed where it touched the lacquered stage.

"Poser," hissed Ren, but Vincent detected a note of envy.

Lady Clore curtsied, sending a ripple through the front rows. A child near the aisle promptly fainted, which delighted her. She extended her fan, wafting the crowd as if bestowing a benediction of subtle doom.

Ashcroft continued, "Our next guest—renowned for his unconventional approach to the Hippocratic oath, and the only man barred from Guy's Hospital for 'excessive zeal'—please welcome Dr Erasmus Pike!"

The second coffin burst open in a spray of splinters. Pike was a stick of a man, all angles and wild eyes, lab coat in tatters, stained with the sorts of things that might once have been organic. His hands were wrapped in surgical gauze, but this failed to conceal the bone saws and rib shears attached at various points up his arms. He grinned, flashing an impossible number of teeth.

Vincent recognised the type. "Bloody hell, it's House, MD if the script was by Clive Barker."

Pike stalked the edge of the stage, bowing to Lady Clore, then to the audience, then to Ashcroft, as if trying to collect the set. "Such excellent specimens!" he crowed, eyes darting. "So many improvements to be made!"

"Does he mean the living or the dead?" asked Ren.

Vincent shrugged. "Probably both. Maybe the seats, too."

Ashcroft relished the chaos. He held for applause, then drew a deep, wholly unnecessary breath.

"And last, but never least—the man whose words damned a century, whose duels rewrote the laws of gentlemanly conduct, whose unfinished verse haunted the entire Royal Society—my fellow in arms, and in arts: Mr Algernon Bleak!"

The third coffin opened not with a bang, but with a gentle click. The man inside was dressed for a funeral, possibly his own: frock coat, cravat, a watch chain looped across his chest. His skin was paper-thin, dusted with blue-black ink, and his hands bore the stains of a thousand broken quills. Instead of eyes, he had fragments of shattered glass glinting in his sockets.

He stepped to the microphone (which was really just a child's karaoke set on a stack of Bibles) and spoke in a voice like an obituary written in wet cement: "I live to be heard, and die to be remembered. Thank you for the second chance."

The applause was scattered at first, then intensified as the audience realised this wasn't performance art, but history returned to bite them on the arse.

Vincent leaned to Ren, whose own Mark had started to itch with a bright, strobing pain. "Wonderful. Britain's worst party guests, back by popular demand."

Ren grimaced. "Can't wait to see the after-party."

On stage, the trio of revenants gathered before Ashcroft, who raised their hands one by one like a championship referee.

"London!" he proclaimed, voice trembling with the joy of a man who'd just set his enemies on fire and blamed it on the weather. "Tonight, you witness the rebirth of greatness. Tomorrow, the world will remember our names. Our stories will never die!"

A cheer, so loud it rattled the rotten ceiling, rose from the crowd. The Modernisers swarmed the front of the stage, phones aloft, already hashtagging the event before it had finished. The mortals shrieked, half in terror, half in ecstasy, as Lady Clore wafted poison mist over the stalls.

Vincent kept his eyes on Ashcroft. The old bastard was soaking in the attention, but underneath, Vincent saw the strain: the flicker of uncertainty, the slight tremor in his left hand as he struggled to hold the narrative together. It was working, for now, but the seams were visible to anyone who'd ever tried to keep a secret alive in this city.

Mrs Barley leaned in, her lips barely moving. "He's built them for a purpose. A trinity—decadence, cruelty, and the word."

Zara nodded. "It's a mythological structure. He's not just summoning monsters, he's seeding a new pantheon."

"London could do better," said Vincent.

"London usually does," said Mrs Barley, "but it's never quick about it."

The stage lights flickered, and for a moment, all three revenants seemed to look directly at Vincent and his entourage. Lady Clore smiled knowingly. Pike flexed his surgical blades. Bleak lifted a hand, ink dripping from his fingers, and pointed at them as if marking them for later.

Ashcroft bowed, once, then twice, then left the stage to thunderous applause. The house lights came up, and instantly the theatre returned to its former decrepitude, but the energy in the air had changed. The night was no longer a passive backdrop, but a living, hungering thing, ready to devour anyone not quick enough to adapt.

As the audience spilled into the street, buzzing with the sort of elation that only follows the realisation that one has just witnessed something deeply illegal, Vincent and the others held back, letting the crush of bodies pass.

Ren stretched, rubbing at the Mark. "That's going to get worse, isn't it?"

"Count on it," said Vincent.

Zara ghosted into the aisle, examining the footprint of magic left on the stage. "He's got a perfect circuit. Every time one of those three causes havoc, the Draft Eternal gets stronger. And so does Ashcroft."

"Lovely," said Mrs Barley, closing her notepad. "And we're the only idiots with a hope of interrupting."

Vincent smiled, tight and cold. "Let's not keep London's new gods waiting, then."

They slipped into the street, the theatre already shuttered behind them, the roar of the departing crowd fading into the sound of emergency vehicles. Above, the city's skyline flickered between now and then, gaslights battling with LEDs, and somewhere in the thickening dark, three old nightmares smiled.

It was, Vincent decided, shaping up to be the worst opening night of his career.

It turned out that the only thing London loved more than a comeback story was a public safety crisis. By the time Vincent and his patchwork squad made it from Curtain's Call to Whitechapel, the night had gone from dramatic to dire.

Ashcroft's three "guests" had wasted no time implementing their debut tour, and within minutes, all of Shoreditch was trending for reasons that would make a serial killer blush.

The trinity of nightmares didn't even try to hide. They flaunted themselves, an anti-royal procession: Lady Euphemia Clore, the arsenic angel, floated into a cocktail bar with the insouciance of a catwalk model; Dr Erasmus Pike set up a triage unit in an alley behind a Shisha lounge; Algernon Bleak stalked the street, reciting extemporaneous poetry at passersby and occasionally shooting at them.

Vincent assessed the map of havoc as Zara projected it in real time onto her phone screen. "We split up," he said. "Classic horror mistake, but better than fighting all three together."

Ren grunted, already scanning the map for the poet. "I'll take Bleak. He looks like he'll fold if someone threatens to punch him in the mouth."

"Mrs Barley?" Vincent looked at the old housekeeper.

"I'll manage the socialite," she said, with the careful diction of a woman who had once contained the aftermath of a poltergeist-fuelled garden party. "I've dealt with worse at book club."

Zara hovered a few paces behind, arms crossed, more solid now than Vincent had ever seen her. "You get the surgeon, then. Try not to let him upgrade you."

Vincent felt a shiver along his vertebrae, but he shrugged it off. "Never fancied elective surgery anyway."

They peeled off, each heading for their target, with Zara as mission control, relaying live updates in a voice that now trembled with static.

The night air was sharp, filled with the distant thump of subwoofers and the closer wail of police klaxons. Vincent pulled up his collar, ducked around a street corner, and nearly tripped over a blood trail leading to Pike's makeshift "clinic."

It was a horror show. Pike had built an operating theatre from milk crates and an ironing board, draped with a bedsheet that had never known bleach. His audience was an unlucky food delivery rider, currently unconscious, with Pike narrating the procedure for a circle of fascinated junkies.

"Observe," Pike intoned, "the delicacy of the humeral artery. Most modern physicians would baulk at such exposure, but I say—let us embrace the possibilities!" He waved a bone saw like a conductor's baton. "Anatomy is but the poetry of the flesh!"

Vincent stifled a laugh, then stepped forward. "Don't let the GMC catch you talking like that. They'll revoke your podcast privileges."

Pike's eyes lit up. "A volunteer! You have the bone structure of a Renaissance sculpture—so much wasted potential." He gestured with a scalpel, bloodless but menacing. "How shall we improve you?"

"Start by improving your bedside manner," Vincent said. He closed the distance, feinting with a left, and then smashed a right hook into Pike's jaw.

It should have ended the fight. Instead, Pike's head snapped sideways, detached from his body, then reattached with a wet click. "Delightful!" he cackled. "You'll make a marvellous experiment."

They circled, exchanging jabs and insults. Pike's hands were everywhere, scalpel slicing, bone saw grinding. Vincent took a cut to the arm, felt the familiar rush of healing kick in, and used the pain to drive a knee into Pike's stomach. The revenant doubled over, then stitched himself shut with a rusted needle, never breaking eye contact.

"You're enjoying this too much," Vincent panted.

Pike shrugged. "Afterlives are dull. You must create your own excitement."

Vincent swept Pike's legs, sending him crashing into the crates. For a moment, the surgeon lay motionless. Then he sprang up, brandishing a rib-spreader.

"I admit," said Pike, "I did not expect such resistance. You are a rare specimen, Mr Lupo. May I have your autograph when we are finished?"

Vincent grinned. "Only if I get to sign your death certificate."

He tackled Pike, pinning him to the ground. With a growl, he snapped the rib-spreader in two and jammed the broken ends into Pike's shoulders, pinning him like a butterfly. Pike writhed, then stilled, laughing.

"Oh, exquisite. I shall remember this always."

Vincent stepped back, wiping blood from his mouth. "You won't have much time to forget it."

The surgeon smiled, teeth like piano keys. "We'll see."

Vincent left him there, knowing the victory would be temporary. He tapped his comm, calling Zara. "One down. Mrs Barley's next."

Mrs Barley approached Lady Euphemia Clore with the composure of someone about to inspect an underperforming dust mop. The socialite had ensconced herself at the bar's best table, holding court over a coterie of influencers and day traders.

Clore tipped her fan at Mrs Barley, eyes cold and appraising. "You're not on the list," she said. "Try the Wetherspoons down the street."

Mrs Barley smiled, unmoved. "Containment protocol, Subsection 7: Hostile Entity Detainment." She produced a folded sheet of parchment, official as a tax bill. "You are hereby instructed to cease and desist all intoxicating activities."

Clore's laughter was pure ice. "Darling, I invented intoxicating activities."

Mrs Barley sidestepped a thrown glass, then another, then caught the third and set it down, never breaking eye contact. "You misunderstand. This is not a negotiation."

Clore snapped her fan shut, revealing a hidden stiletto. "Then we shall do this the old way."

They circled, patrons scattering. Clore flicked the blade in elegant arcs, each one missing by less than a hair. Mrs Barley moved with unhurried precision, her every step designed to corral Clore toward the emergency exit.

"Bureaucrats bore me," Clore hissed.

"That's our job," said Mrs Barley. She caught the next lunge, redirected it, and locked Clore's arm behind her back in a grip that would have impressed a professional bouncer.

"You're not even a vampire," Clore spat.

"No," Mrs Barley agreed, "but I am extremely stubborn."

Clore writhed, but Mrs Barley held firm. "You're not the

only one who can play dead," she whispered, then clapped a binding glyph onto Clore's back. The revenant screamed as the magic took hold, freezing her in place.

Mrs Barley brushed off her hands, then nodded at the onlookers. "Show's over. Please tip your bartender."

Ren found Bleak in Hoxton Square, holding forth to an audience of empty bins and three terrified interns. He paced, pistol in one hand, book of verse in the other, alternating between recitals and random shots fired into the air.

"Time is a wheel," he declared, "and we are the spokes! Revolving, returning, doomed to break or bend!" He fired off a round, which ricocheted and took out a streetlight. "Such is the poetry of existence!"

Ren stalked up, fists clenched. "Your metaphors are shit," she called.

Bleak stopped, cocked his head. "A critic! How delightful. Shall we duel?"

"Only if you're scared to lose," Ren said, closing the gap.

"Never," Bleak replied, tossing aside the book and aiming the pistol at her chest. "Final words?"

"Not really," said Ren, and charged.

Bleak fired twice. Both shots missed—barely. Ren tackled him, sending them both tumbling to the ground. Bleak was stronger than he looked, and fast. He rolled on top, pressed the pistol to her head, but Ren twisted, knocking the gun aside. It fired, sending up sparks.

Bleak switched tactics, clawing at her with ink-stained hands, trying to smother her with the pages of his own poetry. Ren felt the words seeping into her skin, like wet tattoos. The Mark on her arm flared, burning through her sleeve.

It hurt more than anything she'd ever felt. Her vision doubled, then tripled, as if a hundred versions of herself were fighting Bleak at once. She gasped, barely able to breathe.

Bleak grinned, teeth leaking ink. "You see now. We are all drafts. Only some are allowed to survive."

Ren howled, threw him off, and staggered away, clutching her arm. The Mark pulsed, alive, crawling up her shoulder toward her heart.

Bleak advanced, but stopped as Zara's ghost materialised between them, more solid than before.

"That's enough," Zara said. Her voice layered, echoing. "She's not your anchor."

"Oh, but she is," Bleak purred. "She's the margin in which I am written."

Zara scowled. "You're a footnote at best. And I always delete the footnotes."

She reached out, touched Bleak's forehead. He howled as a spectral light shot through him, peeling away the layers of ink and bone, leaving only a faint afterimage behind.

Ren collapsed against a bin, Mark still burning. "They're... connected to me," she gasped.

Zara knelt by her side, smoothing the air around Ren's face. "I'm sorry. It's worse than I thought."

Ren blinked up, sweat stinging her eyes. "What do you mean?"

Zara's ghost flickered. "Ashcroft's not just reviving old

monsters. He's using the Draft Eternal to bind them to living threads. You're one. Vincent's another. Maybe even Mrs Barley."

Ren tried to stand. "So what, we're batteries? Narrative batteries?"

"Anchors," Zara said softly. "If you go down, the story sticks. Forever."

The city wailed in the distance, the sound of fresh sirens and the panicked tweets of a hundred thousand witnesses. Ren's phone buzzed with alerts: "Weird gas at the Old Blue Last," "Street magician kills it in Hoxton," "Is East London haunted?"

She managed a laugh, bitter and bright. "We're trending."

Zara helped her to her feet. "Let's find the others. We need to regroup."

They found Vincent and Mrs Barley waiting at the agreed checkpoint, each looking more battered than before. Mrs Barley had a cut above her eyebrow, but her expression was serene. Vincent's knuckles were raw, but he was grinning.

"We've been promoted to existential threat," he said.

"Congratulations," muttered Ren. "What's the next step?"

Mrs Barley dabbed her brow with a monogrammed handkerchief. "We take the fight to Ashcroft. Break the chain before he can write it into history."

Zara nodded, her outline flickering like a dying neon sign. "The longer we wait, the more he'll bring across. London will drown in its own monsters."

Vincent looked around at his battered crew. "No pressure, then."

They started walking, the city shifting and groaning around them. In the alleys, shadows moved, and in the pubs, history rewrote itself by the pint.

# FIVE

Vincent had never trusted dark alleys, not even before the city's recent descent into madness. London's veins had always run with piss, chip wrappers, and the wretched optimism of lost revellers, but now the backstreets had something extra: a sense of narrative purpose, as if they'd been drafted in as extras for a film where all the best roles went to psychopaths.

Tonight, the Mark on Ren's arm drew them off Spitalfields Market with the conviction of a satnav programmed by a poltergeist. It pulsed beneath her sleeve like a tiny, angry lighthouse, the skin around it slick with sweat despite the night's chill. She walked ahead of Vincent, head down, the angle of her shoulders warning off even the most determined muggers.

The alley itself stank of wet paper and deep-fat frying oil, its puddles illuminated by the conflicting neon of a vape shop and a twenty-four-hour pawnshop. The lights fought each other in sickly blue and emergency-vehicle red, the combined effect making every face look guilty and every shadow a probable crime scene. Vincent followed, hands deep in his coat pockets, eyes flicking from the bin bags to the slowly congealing pools of indeterminate origin underfoot.

Ren didn't slow until they reached the dead end, a stretch of wall so thoroughly fly-posted it looked like it had survived three separate revolutions. She hesitated, then pointed. "There," she whispered, and Vincent's gaze slid past her to the makeshift tableau at the alley's heart.

A rickety trestle table, its top warping under the weight of a man strapped down with belts, wire, and what looked suspiciously like the missing leads from a council CCTV junction box. The man's face was raw with terror, his body jerked with each effort to break free, but the restraints held—tight enough to bite.

Kneeling at the foot of the table, Dr Erasmus Pike was a portrait of professional mania. His coat, once an NHS standard-issue, now bristled with stitched-on pockets and glinted with the promise of amateur surgery. His hands, impossibly long and splayed, worked with calm efficiency at the victim's shin, where the flesh was already peeled back in a parody of anatomy textbook diagrams. Each time Pike's rusted clamp bit down, the patient's scream rebounded off the alley walls and up into the glittering night.

Vincent saw the surgeon's face in three stages: first, the hard glint of a monocle, cracked through and fogged with old blood; next, the fixed, rictus smile that had got Pike fired from at least two hospitals; finally, the lines of excitement around his mouth, as if this was the highlight of his week and he was desperate not to miss the denouement.

Vincent leaned in to Ren, his own voice little more than a

ghost of a snarl. "Finally, a doctor who makes NHS waiting lists look merciful."

She didn't laugh. He didn't expect her to.

He stepped forward, shoes splashing, and called out, "Evening, Dr Pike. This a walk-in, or do you accept referrals?"

Pike looked up, hands still pressing a bone saw to the shuddering leg, and his lips stretched wider. "Ah! Mr Lupo. I was hoping for an upgrade, but I suppose your bones will have to suffice."

He abandoned his victim, rising in a whip-crack motion that defied physics and polite society both. The bone saw came with him, slick with arterial spray. He advanced, the motion eerily smooth, eyes fixed not on Vincent's face but his clavicle—as if already mapping out the precise entry point for the blade.

Vincent felt his heart kick in, more out of professional rivalry than fear. He let Pike get close, close enough that the surgeon's breath brushed his cheek and the stench of blood, formalin, and old cigarillos registered as a physical force. At that range, Pike's voice was a brittle rasp: "Let's see what you're made of, Vincent. I do hope it's something rare."

Vincent didn't give him the satisfaction. He snapped his left hand up, catching the saw by its back edge. The teeth grated across his palm, carving shallow furrows that ached but did not bleed—not yet. His right fist followed, catching Pike under the chin with enough force to snap the monocle's chain and send the lens spinning into the gutter.

Pike staggered back, swiping at Vincent with the blade, but this time Vincent parried with his forearm, letting the serrated edge bite deep, then wrenching it sideways. The surgeon shrieked, less in pain than in gleeful anticipation, and lashed out with the free hand, catching Vincent at the jawline with a set of fingers more bone than skin.

Ren hissed behind him. The Mark on her arm shone now, visible even through the grime of her hoodie. Vincent saw the blue fire reflect in Pike's eyes, and for a moment, they both froze, mesmerised by the pulse of living prophecy.

That was all the opening Vincent needed. He twisted the bone saw free, reversed his grip, and drove it towards Pike's stomach. The blade slid in with a noise like shears through wet cardboard. Pike's mouth opened, closed, then opened again as he regarded the new wound with admiration.

"Magnificent," he gasped, and began to stitch the wound closed with the needle and thread he kept ready in his sleeve. His hands moved so fast, Vincent barely saw the thread until it cinched tight and knotted, the fresh cut already mended by the time Pike straightened.

Vincent grunted. "You always were a quick study, Doctor."

Pike grinned. "Some of us learn on the job." He lunged again, this time with the full force of a revenant unchained, and the two of them slammed into the alley wall. The bricks shook; a nearby window rattled in its frame.

Above, a cold shape drifted through the lamplight—Zara, watching, her ghost-light face serene and unreadable. At the table, Mrs Barley had wasted no time. She knelt by the captive, her hands working at the bindings with all the delicacy of a bomb squad technician. Each time the man moaned, she murmured words so soft they vanished into the alley's wet air. Her focus was absolute, as if she'd trained for this precise moment in the basement of some secret MI5 branch office.

Vincent felt the pressure on his throat as Pike pressed

harder, the surgeon's eyes wild with delight. "You should let go, Mr Lupo. It's so much easier when you stop struggling."

Vincent spat, the bloody phlegm catching Pike in the eye. "Never liked shortcuts."

He rammed his knee up, hard, and Pike doubled over, gasping. Vincent caught him by the collar and spun, pinning him against the wall. He raised the bone saw for a final cut—but Pike slipped free, oiled by his own blood, and scampered crabwise up the bricks, leaving a smearing trail of red-black behind him.

Ren, at the alley's mouth, clutched her arm, nails biting so deep they left crescent moons. "He's not done," she muttered. "None of them are."

Vincent heard the warning, ducked just as Pike dropped from above, and caught the surgeon's ankle mid-fall. They tumbled together into a heap of bin bags and broken glass, scrabbling for leverage. Pike's hands darted, pinched, and in a moment of pure horror, he tried to gouge out Vincent's eye with his thumb.

Vincent bit down on the thumb, hard, felt the brittle snap of bone, and spat the tip out onto the concrete. Pike howled, fell back, and finally, for the first time, looked unsure.

Vincent advanced, slow. "We're done here, Doctor."

Pike stared at him, then at Ren, then at the table where Mrs Barley had freed the patient and was wrapping a sheet around the ruined leg. Above, Zara hovered, face now fully luminous, her gaze pinning Pike in place.

Pike looked up, grinned with bloodied teeth, and whispered, "You've no idea what's coming. I was just the warm-up."

He slammed the back of his head against the wall, once, twice, three times. On the third, his skull caved in like a dropped melon, splattering the bricks with a Rorschach of narrative collapse. Pike's body slid to the ground, still twitching, then stilled.

Vincent wiped his mouth, wiped his hands, and turned to Mrs Barley. "How's our patient?"

She regarded him, eyebrows lifted. "He'll live. Which is, under the circumstances, something of a shock."

Ren slid to the wall, breathing hard, the Mark now faded to a dull ache. She watched Vincent with a mixture of gratitude and horror.

Vincent straightened, tried to stretch the pain out of his back, and managed a grin. "First round's on me."

No one laughed. Even Zara's ghost looked sombre.

They left the alley together, dragging the survivor and leaving the carnage for the council's morning shift. Vincent glanced back only once, to see if Pike would rise for an encore. He didn't. But the feeling in the air—the sense of being watched, of history warping underfoot—didn't leave.

Ren's Mark flickered, once, like a dying bulb. The message was clear: This wasn't an ending. Not even close.

# SIX

The Modernisers kept their headquarters in a repurposed Shoreditch loft, the kind of open-plan sweatshop that had once been a textiles warehouse but now ran on vape pens, overpriced oat milk, and the crushed dreams of failed content creators. Vincent and his crew reached the building just before midnight, the street outside pulsing with enough LED signage to give a migraine to a corpse. The ground floor—originally reception, now a shared workspace for minor bloodsuckers and the odd aspiring TikTok chef—was deserted, save for a single receptionist who blinked at them with the sullen air of a very bored hallucination.

Vincent led the way, Mrs Barley and Ren at his heels, Zara's ghost drifting several steps behind, blue-bright and utterly unimpressed by the architectural pretensions. He'd been here before, of course, but never sober, and the building always found a new way to annoy him.

Tonight, it was the lift. A transparent, reinforced plastic

box, its walls scrawled with glowing graffiti that oscillated between threats of violence and invitations to microdose, waiting for them at the end of a corridor lined with motivational posters. Vincent ignored the "Disrupt the Suck" slogan and stabbed the button. The lift arrived with a pneumatic sigh, then paused as if expecting a tip.

Inside, the lift played a thirty-second promo loop for a "Blood Smoothie" franchise, with a platinum-haired model slurping viscous red from a biodegradable straw. The background beat—something between grime and Gregorian chant—drilled through the box and into Vincent's skull. Ren started humming along, just to annoy him.

Mrs Barley read the scrolling legal disclaimer at the bottom of the lift screen: "Does not cure sunlight allergy. May contain traces of nuts." She pursed her lips. "At least they're honest about their supply chain."

Zara floated up beside Vincent, arms crossed, and eyebrow arched. "Do you ever get used to this?"

Vincent shook his head. "You either die in the Council, or live long enough to see yourself in a start-up's PR loop."

The lift opened at the fifth floor into a world calculated to offend: drones zipped overhead, trailing scents of burnt rubber and artisanal incense; the walls throbbed with neon banners displaying hashtags in gothic font (#VAMPLORE, #THRIVEOFFLINE, #FEEDTHEBRAND); and every surface not already occupied by a ring light had been colonised by high-gloss mock-ups of new vampire merchandise.

At the centre of this consumerist nightmare, a conference table of recycled glass and coffin wood had been arranged as the altar of a cult. Around it, three figures held court, each one a lesson in evolutionary branding.

Aurelia Voss—statuesque, platinum mane arranged in a wave so mathematically precise it could have anchored the Millennium Bridge—reclined in a Danish designer chair. She held a crystal goblet filled with blood and what looked like two fingers of Beluga vodka. At that exact moment, she was livestreaming a skincare routine, her phone balanced in a gold-plated tripod. Her skin, already flawless, glimmered beneath the ring light, and she spoke into the camera with the gentle conviction of someone who knew her entire audience would murder for her opinions.

To her left, Cass Roe perched on the edge of the table, his hoodie emblazoned with a lurid startup logo: "FANGR." He had two phones, three power banks, and a vape pen all in constant rotation. When he spoke, it was at a volume intended to be overheard by everyone, even the deaf. He was currently pitching an "unprecedented, fully-immersive vampire dating app experience" to an unseen livestream audience, pausing every ten seconds to hit his vape or blast out a synthetic cackle.

On the far side, Nyx Calder hunched over a set of DJ decks —actual, physical decks, but with enough arcane circuitry woven through them that Vincent suspected they'd crash the grid if plugged into a regular socket. Nyx's face was obscured by a fall of dark hair and a set of blackout contact lenses; his hands moved with the restless compulsion of a man building his own nervous system from raw bass. He muttered to himself, sometimes in English, sometimes in languages Vincent recognised only from curses scrawled in Roman catacombs.

The whole scene was so perfectly, hideously Moderniser

that Vincent nearly turned around. Instead, he nudged Ren, who was eyeing a rack of "Vegan Plasma" mocktails with what might have been interest or a low-level death wish.

Ren took it in, gave a soft snort. "It's like Hell got a pop-up bar in Soho."

Vincent shook his head. "Behold, the apocalypse in skinny jeans."

Aurelia saw them then, and without breaking her monologue, flashed a smile sharp enough to cut glass. "Darlings!" she trilled, voice pitched to carry through three parallel conversations. "Lupo the Lightless, in my studio! If you told me I'd see you in anything less than a three-piece suit, I'd have called it a hate crime."

Cass Roe looked up, spotted the arrivals, and grinned. "Oh shit, it's the Council's own liability clause! Welcome to the future, mates." He immediately pointed his phone at Vincent, streaming the encounter for whoever cared enough to watch.

Nyx raised one hand in greeting, then stabbed at his deck and conjured a loop of cathedral bells, distorted into something that set Vincent's teeth vibrating.

Vincent strode up to the conference table, but didn't take a seat. "You're all looking well," he said. "Considering the city's about to be a live-fire exercise in narrative collapse."

Aurelia set down her goblet, dabbed her lips with a silk handkerchief, and killed her camera feed in one practiced flick. "You flatter us," she purred. "Is this a social call, or are you here to pitch us on the end of days?"

Ren snorted, plopped herself into the seat next to Cass, and immediately began swiping through the FANGR prototype, her face set to "deeply unimpressed."

Mrs Barley hung back by the door, notebook out, already compiling a list of possible health and safety violations.

Zara's ghost drifted overhead, blue-white and silent, which Aurelia clocked with only a moment's hesitation.

Cass Roe brandished his phone in Vincent's face. "Say hi to the fans, mate. You're trending already."

Vincent batted the phone away with the back of his hand; it spun, then clattered across the polished concrete floor. The livestream audience, or whatever digital ghouls watched these things, would be left to wonder what happened next.

"Sorry," Vincent said. "It's been a long night."

Aurelia made a noise halfway between a laugh and a mew, then leaned in, all business. "Cut to the chase, darling. We're not going to join a Council suicide pact unless you're offering shares, or at least naming rights."

Nyx adjusted the crossfader, muttered "No one survives the final edit," and let the cathedral bells fade into a discordant whine.

Vincent leaned against the Modernisers' glass altar, arms folded, voice pitched for maximum dread. "You all watched the stream. Ashcroft went full Blood-and-Thunder on the Council, killed an Elder, and rewrote the rules. The Draft Eternal's bleeding through every revenant, every idiot with a grudge and a hashtag."

Mrs Barley stepped forward, and fixed the Modernisers with a look so calm it sucked the air out of the room. "If the Draft Eternal rewrites everything, there won't be an audience left to sell to."

Aurelia pursed her lips, eyes narrowed. "You think this is

existential for us? Honey, the only thing that ever threatened us was irrelevance."

Ren, still playing with the app, piped up: "You want legitimacy. This is your chance. Save the world and even the Council has to take you seriously."

Cass perked up, running the numbers in his head like a rat in a cocaine maze. "The PR would be insane. Hashtag: Vampire Apocalypse Squad. We could sell tickets to the resistance."

Nyx hummed under his breath, then said: "The city's always been written by liars. Might as well pick a side."

Aurelia's smile returned, this time with actual warmth behind it. "Fine, Lupo. You want the Modernisers? You've got us. On one condition—visibility. We don't get folded back into the footnotes after you save the day, like after Carmine."

Vincent groaned, pinched the bridge of his nose. "Fine. But if anyone turns this into a meme, I walk."

Zara's voice, dry as the London air at four a.m., filtered down from above. "Too late. They already did."

Cass's phone, miraculously undamaged, began to ping with new notifications. #VampireApocalypseSquad was trending.

Vincent looked at Ren, who looked back with the weary resignation of a woman who had seen every flavour of idiocy the city had to offer, and still cared enough to call it out.

"Let's get on with it, then," he said, and watched as the Modernisers, the ghosts, and the last of his own patience settled in for the war.

# SEVEN

Vincent had seen his share of mausoleums, but the Mayfair townhouse took top prize for posthumous dedication to a colour scheme. From pavement to pediment, the building radiated a jaundiced glow, its Portland stone now the shade of a nicotine patch. Only the brass plate by the door, burnished to the point of religious mania, offered any concession to the present century.

He paused at the entrance, eyeing the elaborate ironwork and the knocker, which looked suspiciously like a human femur cast in bronze. "Subtle," he muttered. "Nothing says 'open mind' like a door that doubles as a warning."

Ren snickered beside him, hands stuffed deep into her hoodie, the only thing keeping her from freezing in the wind. "Maybe they're just into paleo aesthetics," she said. "You ever seen so many white columns in one place?"

Mrs Barley, immune to both sarcasm and cold, pressed the

bell with a gloved finger. The chime was more an accusation than a welcome, echoing through the vestibule and up a staircase wide enough to accommodate the entire cast of an Edwardian sitcom.

The door opened to reveal a butler, his suit so precisely starched it threatened to draw blood. He inspected Vincent and the others with the polite contempt of a man who had once catered for actual royalty, and now had to admit ghostly hangers-on and council troublemakers as a condition of continued employment.

"This way, please," he intoned, with the certainty of someone who could and would report trespassers to the appropriate authorities—if not the police, then the National Trust.

The corridor beyond was a slow-motion car crash of every century's worst interior design choices: the panelling was dark, the carpeted runner lighter only by contrast, and the walls sagged under the weight of ancestral portraits in gilt frames the size of family hatchbacks. Each face glared down with some combination of madness, bad dentistry, and an apparent vendetta against anyone not named "Mortimer" or "Honoria."

Vincent trailed his hand along the banister, then regretted it —the varnish still sticky from the last restoration. "You'd think for all the money they spend, they could afford a dehumidifier," he whispered to Ren.

She gave him a side-eye. "Some people pay extra for 'atmosphere.'"

Mrs Barley shushed them with a look, and the party entered the main salon. If the corridor was the warning shot, the sitting room was the artillery.

It was a cube of sepia, every surface flocked or papered or otherwise upholstered in something at least seventy years out of date. A chandelier dangled like a threat from the ceiling, the candles real and already oozing wax onto the carpet. On the far wall, a fire blazed in an enormous hearth, the flames more for effect than heat.

Arranged around the fireplace were three Traditionalist elders, each one a specimen of a very particular breed of undead aristocracy. They wore their lineage like a badge—morning coats, ascots, shoes shined to a mirror finish, not a hair or whisker out of place. All that was missing was a Victorian undertaker to pronounce the hour.

The first, a heavy-browed man in a dove-grey frock coat and silk cravat, rose as they entered. He gripped a cane with a silver wolf's head for a handle and studied Vincent as if expecting him to be housebroken. "Council's contractors arrive at last," he drawled. "Punctuality, I see, remains an aspiration rather than a custom."

Vincent tried to smile, but it came out more as a demonstration of dental health. "We had to stop for snacks. Some of us aren't on the liquid diet."

Ren choked back a laugh, which earned her a look from the third elder—an imperious woman with a neck long enough to warrant a giraffe's jealousy, all bound up in high-lace collar and cameo brooch. She sat rigidly in her chair, gloved hands clasped over a lapdog that regarded the newcomers with naked loathing.

The second man, smaller and wiry, wore a waistcoat of such savage yellow that Vincent's vision blurred around its edges. He checked a pocket watch, snapped it shut with a noise like a gunshot, and said, "You will understand that we convene only under protest. Our custom does not admit of coalition with... with—" He groped for a word, found only a sneer, "—parasites in sequins."

Mrs Barley did not rise to the bait. Instead, she took her seat with the calm of a woman who had once sedated a rabid dog with nothing but a disapproving glare. "The situation is urgent. Lord Ashcroft—"

The woman's lips thinned. "—was a guest in this house, twice, and comported himself as a gentleman both times. Unlike some, he respects tradition. If you are here to defame his name, I shall ask you to reconsider your line of approach."

Ren, who had been ogling the chandelier, said, "He killed a council elder on livestream. Is that traditional? Or is that a new innovation?"

The elders shifted, discomfort rippling through the fabric of their collective dignity. The first man tapped his cane on the hearth. "Dueling law is explicit. The Council was given ample warning, and the challenge was delivered in accordance with every article. Blackthorn's demise, while... regrettable, was entirely by the book."

"Right," Vincent said, "because murder's always fine if you file the right paperwork first."

The yellow-vested man glared. "You wouldn't understand. You have no history."

Vincent grinned, displaying all of it at once. "I'm seven hundred years old. I have more history than you've had hot dinners."

The room chilled, or perhaps the wind found a new way

through the cracks. In the silence, the tick of a grandfather clock by the door grew to fill the space, counting down to the next polite outrage.

Mrs Barley produced a folder from her briefcase. "The Council requests your support in containing the current outbreak. If Ashcroft succeeds, he will destabilise not only the Council but every line of inheritance and privilege upon which your position depends."

The woman stroked the lapdog, which bared its teeth at Vincent. "We are not children. We know the stakes. But the Modernisers—" she spat the word like a curse, "—are unreliable. They would sell the city for a month's worth of headlines."

Vincent shrugged. "Better than selling it for a seat at a table that's already on fire."

The elders bristled. Even the lapdog looked scandalised.

Ren, emboldened, added, "Let's be honest, the world's ending. Maybe time to try something new."

The cane tapped again, slow and deliberate. "Young lady, the world ends and begins every generation. The only difference is who gets to write the obituary."

Vincent rolled his eyes, and leaned toward Ren, keeping his voice low but not that low. "Perfect. The Titanic's sinking, and they're still arguing over deckchair arrangements."

At this, the monocle of the yellow-vested elder actually popped out, landing with a delicate tink on the tray beside him. He retrieved it with the precision of a man for whom indignation was a way of life.

The woman shot Vincent a look so cold it could have refrozen the Thames. "If you have nothing further to propose, Mr Lupo, we shall take our chances with the old ways."

"Fine by me," Vincent said, rising from his chair. "But if Ashcroft rewrites the city into a penny dreadful, don't expect the rest of us to stick to your script."

"If I may, ladies and gentlemen," Mrs Barley stopped at the doorway. "There is precedent. If I might suggest we discuss over brandy."

"Fine." Lady Malady answered for the group. "But should we not be convinced, you shall be cast out of here like the vagabonds you are."

The sitting room was even chillier than the dining room, as though the ancestral portraits had dialled down the heating in protest. The three elders settled into their favourite chairs and reluctantly indicated for the visitors to join them.

Vincent and Ren took their seats on the settee, which had been designed for maximum discomfort. Mrs Barley stood at a sideboard, gloved fingers trailing over the decanters as if considering which to weaponise. The lapdog barked incessantly.

Mrs Malady shushed the lapdog with a brittle "Hush, Cerberus," then fixed Mrs Barley with a stare that could have stripped wallpaper. "We have reviewed the Council's request," she said, "and find it lacking in both courtesy and precedent."

The yellow-vested elder, picked up the thread: "You invoke emergency statute, yet the definition of 'emergency' has always been subject to the approval of the hereditary courts. To bypass this is not just irregular—it is subversion."

Vincent arched a brow. "You'd rather wait for the world to end, then take a vote?"

"It is the only civilised way," the man insisted.

The argument spiralled, as predicted, into a pageant of pettiness. Ren counted at least four digressions into obscure ritual, two recitations of genealogical superiority, and a running side-debate about whether duelling law permitted formal truces. Vincent didn't bother to hide his yawns.

Mrs Barley, meanwhile, waited.

She waited through the first volley of objections, the second, and the entire digression into the time one ancestor had briefly usurped the Hungarian throne by creative interpretation of feudal jurisdiction. Only when the yellow-vested man (now definitely in mourning attire, which Vincent decided to call "coup-casual") leaned forward to cite the Council's own regulations back at her did Mrs Barley act.

She clicked open the briefcase.

The sound was so sharp that even the lapdog flinched. From the case, she withdrew a stack of documents, each one banded in red tape and stamped with an array of seals that would have given any notary a small aneurysm.

"If I may," she said, and spread the documents with an elegance that made Ren's jaw pop. "Council Regulation 473, paragraph three: 'In the event of narrative instability, and upon threat of existential breach, all Houses are compelled to comply with emergency coalition—'"

"Only if ratified by—" the yellow-vested man began, but Mrs Barley cut him off with the flick of a page.

"Appendix B, subclause nine, as amended 1871 and reconfirmed by the Schopenhauer Compromise of 1962: 'The ratification process is considered moot when two or more of the following conditions are met: loss of quorum, manifestation of Class Three narrative hazard, or direct invocation of the Draft Eternal by a Council member.'"

She pointed to the relevant line, then looked up, her voice

now a shade sharper: "All three have occurred, gentlemen. And madam."

The cane thudded onto the carpet. The room's silence was of the deadliest sort.

Mrs Barley continued: "Refusal to participate in such an emergency is, by precedent, not merely dereliction of duty but —" here she paused for effect, "—grounds for charges of high treason against the Council and, by extension, the city."

The monocle did not just fall this time. It ricocheted off the side table and landed in a glass of brandy with a plop so audible that even Vincent felt the urge to applaud.

Lady Malady inhaled as if to protest, but Mrs Barley produced the clincher: a battered leather-bound volume of duelling precedents, its spine reinforced by several generations of dried blood.

"Duelling precedent 1212, the Mortlake Protocol," Mrs Barley read, "stipulates that in any challenge resulting in the death of a sitting Elder, all disputes over legitimacy must be suspended pending resolution of the existential threat. In other words: if Ashcroft wins, he decides what comes next. Not you."

The cane rattled in the elder's grip. "But... but he is a traitor—"

"Which is exactly why you must oppose him," Mrs Barley said. "Otherwise, by the Council's own law, he is the only legitimate authority left standing."

Vincent grinned, delighted. He looked over at Ren, whose eyes were wide, then back at the elders. "You see? The world's not going to be saved by fangs and capes. It's going to be saved by paperwork."

The silence stretched until the clock chimed the hour.

Then the yellow-vested man, white as parchment, nodded with all the solemnity of a man attending his own burial. "If the world must be saved," he said, "let it at least be done properly."

The others, Lady Malady included, gave curt bows of the head. The lapdog, perhaps sensing the changing of the guard, slunk under the table to sulk.

Mrs Barley collected the documents, then snapped the briefcase closed with a finality that was almost smug. "We'll see you at the rally point, then," she said.

Vincent and Ren followed her out, Zara's ghost joining them in the corridor, blue-bright and more animated than Vincent had seen her in weeks.

"That was..." Ren managed, searching for the word.

"Brutal," said Vincent. "Exquisite."

Mrs Barley gave the tiniest shrug. "I used to run an estate in Wiltshire. This is nothing compared to the annual AGM."

Zara shimmered with glee. "I think you broke them so thoroughly, they'll have to join the Modernisers just to restore their sense of grievance."

Vincent laughed, high and sharp. "All hail the new alliance —bound by mutual loathing and Council subclauses."

They stepped into the night, the Mayfair house behind them already sealing up its secrets, its ancestors perhaps rolling in their frames.

"Do you think they'll show?" Ren asked.

Vincent considered, then nodded. "They have to. Their own rules are now a suicide note."

Mrs Barley checked her watch, then smiled. "Plenty of time, then. Shall we?"

They walked on, the city's lights ahead, Zara's ghost flickering bright with every step. Behind them, the old world tottered, propped up only by the weight of its own regulations—and, Vincent suspected, a growing sense of existential dread.

But that was someone else's problem.

Tonight, the present was in session, and they had a war to win.

# EIGHT

The Council's emergency chamber had been requisitioned from the highest bidder, which, given the Council's present liquidity crisis, meant it was an over-lit, under-cleaned function room at the back of the Museum of Legal Curiosities. The only concession to vampire aesthetics was the ironwood table—three times too long, burnished to a coal-black sheen, and scarred in places where generations of governance had misjudged the tensile strength of both wood and resolve.

Tonight, it played host to a coalition meeting that could only have been convened under circumstances of maximum desperation. Down the left-hand side, Modernisers in lanyards and branded hoodies, each posture calculated for maximum affront. Opposite, the Traditionalists: starched, powdered, glaring out from above cuffs and collars that cost more than most minor inheritances. At the centre, the "neutral party": Vincent, Ren, Mrs Barley, and the spectral Zara, who hovered at ceiling height, radiating the energy of a ghost watching a very slow car crash.

The two factions eyed each other as if waiting for the other to blink, or die, whichever came first.

Vincent scanned the room, weighing each present liability. The Modernisers had sent their core: Aurelia Voss—Queen of the Instagrammortal, already streaming live from her phone, nails flashing like knives in the fluorescents; Cass Roe, the startup degenerate, who looked like he'd been awake for a week and survived entirely on novelty energy drinks and illegal supplements; and Nyx Calder, who hunched at the far end, feeding a drip of audio from the room into a set of DJ decks, every so often punctuating the air with a random sample.

The Traditionalists had gone for spectacle: at least three elders, each so embalmed by vanity they looked embalmed for real, plus a coterie of lesser hangers-on, all lined up by descending order of relevance. The leader was a white-haired man who could have passed for a badly-restored marble bust, complete with a jawline sharpened by centuries of disuse and a signet ring big enough to cosh a medium-sized sheep. He had a cane, and made sure everyone noticed it, rapping it against the table each time he wanted attention, which was constantly.

Vincent sat back, scanned for exits, and wondered what the odds were on at least two murders before the hour.

Mrs Barley, by contrast, had set herself up as the event's secretariat: notepad open, pen poised, lips pursed in the international symbol for "We're not leaving here until we get an agreement." Ren sprawled in her seat with the relaxed composure of someone who'd spent a lifetime ignoring any form of official protocol. Every so often she'd glare at her phone, then at the room, as if comparing the awfulness of both and not liking the result.

Zara's ghost took a place above the centre, where the room's acoustic design was at its worst. She was more solid tonight, blue aura flaring every time the tension in the room spiked, which was often. Occasionally, her lips would move in a running commentary only Vincent could hear, and he resented her for enjoying the spectacle so much.

The first five minutes were a silent arms race in posturing. The Modernisers fired up their ring lights and began synchronised "group selfie" routines, ignoring the Traditionalists entirely. The Traditionalists responded by pretending the Modernisers didn't exist, instead holding whispered debates about which ancestor would have found this situation the most disgraceful.

Vincent watched Aurelia snap a filtered, pouting photo of the whole table, add the hashtag #FutureFangs, and then set her phone to record.

The Traditionalist leader finally made a show of checking his pocket watch, a gesture so pointed it might as well have come with footnotes. He thumped his cane and intoned, "Let us proceed. Some of us keep time by means other than the electronic tick of distraction." His tone was a thing of purebred contempt, intended to wound.

Aurelia batted her lashes. "If you prefer, I can have my PA send over the transcript. Or I can just summarise—'old men moan, new world wins, get used to it.'"

The cane thudded again. "We begin with the matter of seating order. Council law is explicit: bloodlines rank before novelties."

Cass, who'd already started a group chat mid-table, snorted. "Mate, the only bloodline you've got left is in your steak tartare. Get over yourself."

Across the aisle, a Traditionalist minor erupted. "This is precisely why the old order stands! Without respect for the forms, we devolve into rabble!"

"Rabble's fun at parties," said Nyx, voice flat and bored. "You ever been to one?"

That drew a ripple of laughter from the Modernisers, who high-fived with the synchronised coordination of a professional e-sports team.

Mrs Barley scribbled a note, then raised a hand. "If we might return to the agenda—?"

The white-haired elder ignored her, instead lurching into a speech about the importance of hierarchy, the sanctity of the chain of command, and the dangers of permitting "unregulated ambition" into positions of power. It was the sort of rhetoric that, in another life, might have presaged a small war, or at least a disastrous dinner party.

Aurelia caught his eye and went for the kill. "You know what kills more vampires than sunlight, darling? Boredom. Maybe try some SPF-50 for the ego, hmm?"

The elder started to retort, but Cass had already angled his phone to capture the bickering, fingers poised for the best screenshot. In the next instant, a hand snaked out and plucked the phone from Cass's grip.

Mrs Barley, in a move so fast it beggared the senses, now held the phone in one hand and a Council-issue security pouch in the other. She placed both on the table with the dignity of an archbishop laying down communion wine.

"No recording," she said, in the same tone she might have used for "No shoes on the carpet." "Council protocol. The matter is confidential."

Cass gaped, momentarily speechless, then looked to Aurelia for support. She shrugged, impressed. "She's good."

Across the table, the Traditionalists straightened waistcoats, adjusted cufflinks, and muttered about "nouveau vampires" and "barbarism." Every few seconds, one of them would attempt to out-sneer the other, producing a symphony of tiny, suppressed snorts.

Vincent's patience, never robust, began to fray. He paced behind his chair, the soles of his boots clicking off the stone, jaw clenching tighter with every circuit.

Aurelia resumed her phone (now in camera-only mode), gesturing for a ring-light refill from her PA, who'd been waiting in the anteroom with the kind of existential resignation that bespoke years of influence-adjacent servitude.

"You know," she announced, "if we spent half as much energy on the actual problem as we do on ancestor cosplay, maybe we'd actually get something done."

The white-haired elder recoiled as if from a bad smell. "Young lady, the problem is that you believe hashtags are a substitute for history."

Ren, who had been mostly silent, grunted. "History's the reason we're all in this room, mate. And it's not working out."

Aurelia, emboldened, leaned in. "I propose—no, I insist—we build a proper brand for this coalition. One with a shared aesthetic. Hashtag: #UnityOrDie. Simple, effective, very now."

A smaller Traditionalist spluttered. "You can't hashtag a war!"

Cass, delighted, retorted, "Not with that attitude."

The room exploded into three simultaneous arguments: one about nomenclature and lineage, one about hashtag etiquette, and one about the relative merits of broadsheet media versus "the algorithmic agora." Every time Mrs Barley tried to interject, the volume only increased, voices ping-ponging off the ironwood and back at twice the force.

Vincent finally snapped. He planted both palms on the table, hard enough to rattle the china and send at least one cufflink spinning across the surface.

"If you children don't stop," he said, fangs half-extended and eyes gone black, "I will stake the lot of you and save Ashcroft the trouble."

It worked. For at least three seconds, the room fell dead silent.

Then, inevitably, Aurelia giggled. "Is this the bit where you spank us and send us to bed without supper? Because I can think of a few followers who'd pay for that content."

Vincent glared at her, then the rest of the room. "You don't have to like each other. In fact, you can loathe each other as much as you please. But if you can't keep your shit together for ten minutes, Ashcroft will rewrite every one of you into a cautionary tale. Understand?"

There was a brief, collective sulk as the Traditionalists smoothed their jackets and the Modernisers exchanged group DMs under the table. Nyx flicked a sample—"Daddy's angry"— through the room, and Ren smirked behind her sleeve.

Above, Zara clapped silently, her hands passing through one another with a faint, cold sparkle. "Not bad," she said, in the echo only Vincent could hear. "You should threaten to eat their phones next."

Mrs Barley, now in possession of Cass's backup device (confiscated during the uproar), cleared her throat. "If I may," she said, once again in her "headmistress to a roomful of arsonists" voice. "The Draft Eternal doesn't care for our politics. If Ashcroft wins, every one of your little hierarchies, and every last follower, will go up in blue smoke. Now—shall we try again?"

For exactly half a minute, Vincent's threat hung in the air like the aftertaste of a bad pun: acrid, lingering, impossible to ignore. But as with all attempts at forced civility, the brief silence soon collapsed under the weight of mutual loathing.

The white-haired elder thudded his cane and intoned, "In my day, threats of bodily harm were delivered in private chambers, not shouted across the people's table." His cronies, emboldened, set about debating whether Vincent's comment should be recorded for posterity or simply referred to a disciplinary subcommittee.

Within seconds, the war of words—and now, petty objects —was back on. A paperclip arced the length of the table, followed by a retaliatory hail of sugar cubes. A Moderniser flung a pen with enough force to embed it in the far panelled wall. The Traditionalists one-upped this by unscrewing the lid from a bottle of centuries-old port and letting it roll, slowly, into enemy territory, where it left a spreading, fragrant stain.

Pens rattled against notepads, chairs scraped and jittered, voices escalated in a fugue of posturing and fury.

Ren, who had watched this arms race with all the patience of a condemned woman on hold with the complaints department, reached a breaking point. Without warning, she slammed both fists on the table—hard enough to silence the room, harder still to leave a hairline crack spidering across the lacquer.

When she spoke, it wasn't a shout, but it scythed through the din with surgical precision. "You want a real story? Here's one."

She jerked up her sleeve, and for the first time since the Mark had claimed her, she put it on open display: from wrist to elbow, the sigil burned not the muted red of an old scar, but a white-blue so intense it lit the veins beneath her skin. It illuminated the underside of her jaw, flared across her cheekbones, and projected fractal, shifting shadows up into the vaults above. For a moment, it painted her as a stained-glass martyr—iconic, and absolutely furious.

She left her arm on the table, let the silence settle in like a chemical spill. The light from the Mark caught the cut glass of the chandelier and refracted it, scattering angry constellations across the wall and the faces of the assembled.

"This," Ren said, voice steady despite the visible tremor in her muscles, "means I'll be the first to die if you all keep dicking about."

She held the gaze of every elder, every influencer, every hanger-on who dared look. "You want to fight over hashtags and seating charts? Fine. But every second you waste, the thing on the other side of this Mark gets closer. I get erased first. After that, it's open season on everyone else in the room."

No one spoke. Not even Aurelia, who had half a joke queued up but lost it to the visual of Ren's arm sparking like a live wire.

Ren looked at the Modernisers. "You wanted a campaign? Make it count. Because when Ashcroft wins, all your followers are gone. Not just unfollowed. Like they never existed."

Then at the Traditionalists: "And you lot—think your ancestors will care if you're the last of your name? Because that's what you'll be. A tombstone. For a bloodline that couldn't adapt."

She sat back down, but the Mark still pulsed, bright as a flare. "So. Decide. Because I'm done being the canary in your coal mine."

Silence settled again, this time longer, rawer. The Traditionalists exchanged glances that weren't quite so smug; the Modernisers lowered their phones, some even looking faintly ashamed. At the far end, Nyx stopped looping the recording, letting the final echo of Ren's words fade out unsullied.

Above, Zara's ghost circled once and then perched, upside down, on a light fitting. "Amazing," she observed to nobody in particular. "Threat of global annihilation? Nothing. One angry teenager with a tattoo? Terrifying."

Vincent, who had spent the entire performance watching Ren with a mixture of dread and something almost like pride, said nothing. But his eyes, when they met hers, were softer than usual—a concession he would never acknowledge out loud.

Mrs Barley, for her part, drew a careful line through the middle of the agenda. "Order of business: forming a plan. All in favour?"

This time, the vote was unanimous. Even the ghosts raised their hands.

83

# NINE

In the unseasonable hour between last train and first, St Pancras International resembled less a transport hub and more the site of a very polite haunting. Vincent stood with his entourage beneath the clock tower, trying to ignore the sensation that history was about to jump the tracks. If the Council's emergency chamber had been a cage, then the station was its parade ground—every arch and pillar dressed for maximum drama in gaslight and LED, old bricks lit from beneath like the jawbone of some palaeolithic beast.

Ren perched on a luggage trolley, swinging her boots and glancing at the departures board, as if hoping the situation might sort itself out if she looked away long enough. Mrs Barley ticked off items on her clipboard with the unflappable precision of a field marshal overseeing a bake sale, while Zara's ghost hovered in the overhead beams, flickering with the blue-white irritability of a fluorescent tube about to give up the ghost.

Vincent checked his watch, then checked it again, as if by

force of will he could delay the inevitable. "Remind me," he said, mostly to himself, "why we're staging the world's most dysfunctional Eurovision in a building designed by someone with a train fetish and zero self-respect."

Ren yawned, unimpressed. "Because it's central, neutral, and nobody wants to risk getting shanked by the Belgians."

Zara's voice filtered down, spectral and bone-dry: "You haven't seen Brussels on a Saturday night. Absolute carnage."

Mrs Barley pursed her lips, as if considering whether to note this for future reference, then said, "Five minutes to arrival. I trust everyone has read the briefing materials?"

Vincent eyed her clipboard. "Unless you've annotated the Treaty of Versailles with a flowchart, I'm not convinced anything in that folder's going to help."

Mrs Barley offered the kind of smile usually reserved for lost children and recalcitrant prime ministers. "One must be prepared. International incidents require a steady hand."

As if summoned by the phrase, the Eurostar train rumbled to the platform, and the German contingent materialised from the North Concourse like the opening volley of a mechanised infantry advance. At their head: Baron Falkenhayn. He was built on the same lines as a vintage tank commander—broad, upright, moustache clipped to a regulation vector, every inch of his dark uniform crisp enough to draw blood. Behind him, three lieutenants marched in lockstep, their boots hitting the flag-stones with enough force to send a shudder through the archi-tecture. Each uniform sported a dazzling array of medals, ribbons, and the kind of metallic insignia usually found on the dashboards of very expensive cars.

They halted at a precise thirty paces, and the Baron offered a bow calculated to communicate both deference and the promise of immediate violence.

"Council representatives," Falkenhayn intoned, voice like a diesel engine idling in a cathedral. "You have my gratitude. Also, my condolences. I trust the arrangements are secure?"

Vincent opened his mouth, but the Baron's gaze shifted to Mrs Barley, who inclined her head and clicked her pen. "All contingencies have been anticipated, Baron. Please remain on the designated platform until the remainder of your party arrives."

Falkenhayn considered this, then nodded, his face unmoving. "Efficiency. Excellent."

Vincent nearly smiled, but the air shifted; somewhere beyond the ticket barriers, a ripple of perfume and panic preceded the arrival of the French delegation.

If the Germans were a marching order, the French were a stage direction. They entered as a block—ten, maybe twelve, strong—like a company of bored ballet dancers on parole. At the centre, Marquis Deveraux swept in, his cloak a velvet thundercloud, his cane more a flourish than a support. The man was blindingly pale, his face a careful confection of powder and shadow, hair slicked back and silvered at the temples for maximum villainy. His entourage matched his hauteur step for step, each wearing some permutation of silk, lace, and centuries-old discontent.

They paused a safe distance from the Germans. For a heartbeat, it was all glances and smirks, the two sides assessing one another as if debating who might taste better roasted. Deveraux made a show of removing his gloves, one finger at a time, then spoke with the languid menace of someone who'd never been told 'no' and didn't intend to start now.

"*Mes amis*," he purred, "how touching to see that the old world still favours punctuality. Baron, it has been—what is the word?—an epoch."

Falkenhayn's lips moved just enough to reveal the possibility of teeth. "Marquis. I see you have not changed your tailor."

"Nor my standards," Deveraux replied. "If I desired a uniform, I would have surrendered at Sedan."

Vincent felt the tension snap tight. "Do we get extra points if someone throws a glove, or does this count as sudden death?"

Ren, never subtle, said, "Could be funnier if they did it in mime."

The French contingent fanned out, the back rank deploying parasols and silk handkerchiefs as if bracing for a gas attack. The Germans responded by aligning their boots and adjusting cuffs. One of Falkenhayn's lieutenants—whose medals threatened to catch the Eurostar's high-beams—cleared his throat, then addressed the room in textbook English.

"Protocol requires us to inquire: Is the Council prepared to guarantee the security of all parties?"

Mrs Barley didn't bother with a smile. "If you would consult page four of your briefing packs, you'll see that St Pancras has been swept for every known hazard, biological or otherwise. The only threats present are standing on this platform."

Deveraux laughed, a brittle, tinkling sound. "She has teeth, this one. I like her."

Zara's ghost hovered lower, drifting between the two camps, her presence drawing a few wary glances from the more superstitious in attendance. She staged a slow, sarcastic round of applause, which only Vincent and Ren seemed to notice.

Falkenhayn snapped his fingers; his retinue tensed, then relaxed as one. "We are ready for the Council's directive."

Vincent stepped forward, flanked by Mrs Barley and Ren. "Right, then. Welcome to London. You'll be working together—yes, together—to prevent the complete narrative collapse of Western civilisation. If you're expecting an official reception, you'll be disappointed. If you're expecting to settle old scores, please schedule it after the main event."

Falkenhayn and Deveraux shared a glance that could have cut glass.

The Marquis flicked imaginary dust from his sleeve. "So, we are to play at coalition. How novel."

"Not so novel," said the Baron. "Your kind has always followed a strong leader. If you lack one, I am available."

Deveraux's smile was all enamel. "Your sense of humour has improved since the Hohenzollerns were in fashion."

Vincent massaged his temples. "Fantastic. We've accidentally booked the Eurovision semifinals."

Ren eyed the French delegation, who had begun ostentatiously ignoring the Germans in favour of one another's company. "Do you think the French actually have any powers, or is it just weaponised flirting?"

Vincent weighed this. "Jury's still out."

The groups maintained their standoff, each drawing the line closer, each trying to stake a claim on the empty platform. Mrs Barley, who could have run a United Nations summit with nothing but a ledger and a bottle of sherry, began distributing colour-coded packets and ushering the visitors toward their designated waiting areas.

She called out, "You will be escorted to Council chambers as soon as the route is clear. Please refrain from inter-delegation altercations until then. Any questions?"

A hand rose from the back of the French ranks—delicate, gloved, unreasonably elegant. "Is there a smoking lounge, madame?"

Mrs Barley didn't blink. "Platform C, third alcove on the left. No open flames."

Deveraux nodded with the solemnity of a man observing a religious rite.

Falkenhayn's number two piped up: "And the armistice lines—are they strictly enforced?"

Ren grinned. "Only if you're scared."

The German bristled, but the Baron cut him off. "We will observe the boundaries, provided the French do not breach them."

Deveraux's eyes twinkled, as if he'd already drawn up several plans for such a breach and committed them to memory in alphabetical order.

Vincent caught Mrs Barley's gaze. "Do you think they'll make it to the chambers without killing each other?"

Mrs Barley checked her clipboard, unruffled. "The risk is minimal. All lethal implements have been declared and tagged."

Vincent's faith in bureaucracy was, for the first time, almost restored.

The hour dragged. The Germans circled like sharks denied a kill, while the French staged an impromptu salon, complete with absinthe flask and what sounded suspiciously like a harpsichord app on someone's phone. Every five minutes, a new round of sniping would break out: the Germans accusing the French of perfidy and cowardice at Waterloo; the French responding with elaborate sighs and cutting references to the inferior tailoring of Prussian uniforms.

After the third such exchange, Vincent slumped onto the bench beside Ren. "What I wouldn't give for just one competent international disaster."

She shrugged. "You get what you pay for."

Zara, perched on the edge of a departure board, leaned over to Vincent's ear and whispered, "Maybe next time, just let them have the war. Might save us some paperwork."

Vincent couldn't argue.

Eventually, Mrs Barley raised her pen and called out, "All delegations: please proceed to the main concourse. The Council is ready for you."

Falkenhayn assembled his party with a barked command; the French responded with a chorus of ironic applause. The two groups set off, side by side, matching strides with the forced politeness of couples walking to a divorce court.

As the teams swept out, the platform fell suddenly, blissfully silent. Vincent watched them go, then turned to his own: Ren, chewing gum and eyeing her phone; Mrs Barley, already drafting the next phase of the plan; Zara, still humming the Eurovision theme.

"We're the adult supervision," he muttered, mostly to himself.

Ren heard, and snorted. "They're all older than you, though."

"Doesn't mean they've grown up."

They gathered their own files and joined the stream of drama headed for Council chambers, the fate of the city (and, with any luck, its supply of decent wine) riding on their ability to keep the world's pettiest monsters from eating each other before breakfast.

If that wasn't heroism, Vincent reflected, he didn't know what was.

The Council had, in its long and disastrous history, hosted any number of international conferences, armistices, and interventions. None had prepared it for the arrival of four fully loaded delegations whose only common trait was the ability to weaponise humiliation as a primary form of communication.

The chamber, once a bulwark of ancient law and dehumidified tradition, was now a patchwork of old-world regalia and the kind of audiovisual kit favoured by teenagers and totalitarian states. The banners of the Traditionalists—stiff with age and possibly actual starch—loomed over their corner of the room, while the Modernisers' side bristled with ring lights, power strips, and the frantic glow of dozens of screens. The Germans set up along the north wall, forming an impromptu Maginot Line with their bodies and briefcases. The French, naturally, took the best seats by the window, arrayed as if waiting for the next revolution to begin.

Vincent slid into the space between, watched as the air charged itself with mutual disdain. On the far side, the Traditionalists had huddled around a single decanter of port, taking slow, deliberate sips and side-eyeing every other group as if expecting them to burst into flames at any moment. Opposite, the Modernisers were already mid-livestream, their followers submitting "hot takes" on international diplomacy at a rate that outpaced most automated spam bots.

The Germans unpacked a full set of files and reference materials within two minutes, then stood behind their chairs at attention, hands folded, and expressions engineered to withstand even the worst continental banter. The French had brought nothing but their egos and, in Deveraux's case, a walking stick so ornate it required a passport.

Mrs Barley entered with the composure of a headmistress breaking up a particularly well-funded food fight. She clapped her hands for attention, which had the effect of a flashbang grenade on the assembled. "All parties, please take your designated seats. I will be distributing materials and outlining the schedule. There will be time for cross-examination and insults after the formalities."

Aurelia Voss, unbothered, snapped a selfie with the German delegation in the background, flashing a peace sign and a set of fangs that had almost certainly never tasted human blood fresh from the source. Baron Falkenhayn flinched as her ring light caught him full in the face, and for a moment it looked as if he might lunge across the aisle and solve the problem with old-fashioned violence.

"Is it necessary," he growled, "to record every moment of this proceeding?"

Aurelia didn't miss a beat. "Only the best ones, darling. My followers expect authenticity."

Deveraux snorted. "If they desired authenticity, they would

subscribe to the Parisian press. Or the German one, for a good laugh."

Falkenhayn's jaw flexed. "You joke now, Marquis, but your kind fled Paris faster than humans flee vampires."

Deveraux spread his hands in mock apology. "It is called *savoir-faire*. Unlike some, we do not celebrate defeat with commemorative stamps."

Cass, emboldened, tried to insert himself. "Actually, Baron, we've got a new app rolling out that would make your entire logistics thing way less tragic. You want to beta test?"

The Baron stared at him, nonplussed. Cass handed over a business card, then a second when the first was not immediately destroyed.

Across the room, the Traditionalists were conducting a low-voiced symposium on whether the French or the Modernisers posed the greater existential threat. The vote was split.

Ren and Vincent took up residence by the chamber's east wall, leaning into the shadow of a bust of Lord Blackthorn, which had been repositioned to face away from the action as a kindness to the dead. Ren watched as the Germans and French rehashed the twentieth century in sixty seconds, then murmured, "Think we could get them to do a musical number? Like West Side Story, but with more fangs?"

Vincent grimaced. "Only if you want the room to catch fire."

Zara's ghost hung near the ceiling, invisible to most but not immune to the drama. She drifted in slow loops, occasionally sticking her tongue out at whichever group seemed to be losing the argument. Every so often, she would pause to mouth an exaggerated 'wow' at some especially tasteless remark.

Mrs Barley, unperturbed, strode from table to table with her trolley of briefing packs. "Traditionalists, these are your colour-coded agendas. You will find the seating chart on the reverse. Please respect the boundaries." She plopped a stack in front of the senior elder, who recoiled as if the plastic cover might bite.

"Modernisers. Yours are on a USB stick and also in the cloud. Wi-Fi password is 'DraftEternal123,' capitals on the D and E. Use it responsibly."

She hit the Germans next, handing over a folder so thick it could have served as body armour. "You are in charge of keeping the minutes. We will provide a translator for the idioms."

The French, last, received a slim binder—leather, monogrammed, with a stylised fleur-de-lis on the front. Mrs Barley smiled at the Marquis, who returned it with a smirk. "You will find the social calendar enclosed, as well as the dietary restrictions. We are aware of your sensitivities."

Deveraux ran a gloved hand over the binder's spine. "Ah, but do you have the wine list?"

"Appendix C," Mrs Barley said.

Vincent watched the factions settle, or try to. Aurelia had stationed herself at the centre, ring light illuminating her like the Statue of Liberty if she'd ever posed for Vogue. She was mid-monologue when a junior German vampire attempted to photobomb; she caught him by the lapel, spun him into frame, and held him there until her phone chirped a successful post.

At the Modernisers' table, Cass had struck up conversation with a pair of French vamps, who responded by pretending not to speak English. Nyx Calder, eyes lidded, remixed the ongoing quarrel into a low, pulsing beat that underscored the entire chamber.

The French and Germans kept up their sniping, the Traditionalists tried (and failed) to reassert control, and the Modernisers continued their social media blitz, prompting one Traditionalist to utter, "They breed like fruit flies, these influencers."

Ren and Vincent observed, neither bothering to hide their boredom. "You know," Ren said, "so far, so good."

Vincent raised an eyebrow. "We've united the vampire world, all right. United in their hatred of each other."

Mrs Barley returned to their side, looking pleased as only a woman with an Excel sheet full of other people's problems could. "We're ready to begin," she said.

"Are we?" Vincent asked.

Mrs Barley nodded. "I have assigned seating, a revised agenda, and a schedule for supervised bathroom breaks. I will not have another Warsaw incident on my watch."

The chamber quieted as Mrs Barley called it to order. She rapped the table once—just loud enough to cut through the muttering and the distant hum of Nyx's soundboard.

"All parties present. The session is open."

Aurelia immediately began to live-tweet.

Falkenhayn stood, the full weight of Prussian dignity behind his words. "We are here in good faith. Let the record show any breach of decorum will be met in kind."

Deveraux fluttered a hand. "As ever, Baron, we are your humble partners. Until the next opportunity arises."

The Traditionalist elder, not to be outdone, stood as well.

"The Council observes, records, and enforces. Let us proceed, and may the best tradition survive."

Vincent exhaled and leaned into the wall, watching as four centuries of grudges, pettiness, and posturing squared off over a conference table. "You know what?" he said to Ren, "Maybe we should just lock them in here and come back in a hundred years."

Ren grinned. "We'd probably still find them arguing."

Above, Zara's ghost winked into visibility, hovered for a moment over the centre of the chamber, and whispered, "Place your bets, gentlemen. Place your bets."

If there was ever a hope for global vampire unity, it was now measured in minutes. But at least, Vincent thought, they were all on the clock.

And that's when they received word that all hell had broken loose in Covent Garden.

# TEN

Even for Covent Garden, the night had got out of hand. The Royal Opera House forecourt, usually a polite scrum of ticket-holders, buskers, and mid-priced pickpockets, now bristled with a far less manageable crowd. Vincent's team spilled from the side street, half Moderniser, half Traditionalist, and all functioning as a walking HR violation. On the steps above, Lady Euphemia Clore stood in full Victorian mourning, commanding a rain of crystal flutes and venomous giggles.

The air stank of fear, cordite, and whatever hellish cocktail the venue had served at intermission. The crowd wasn't just panicked; it was in the process of self-dismantling, bodies collapsing onto the marble in spasms, limbs flailing in operatic gestures as champagne-induced agony found new outlets for expression. What hadn't been designed as immersive theatre was rapidly becoming so, with tourists filming on their phones, convinced they'd scored front-row seats at the next big viral sensation.

Vincent paused, scanning the steps. The old predatory instinct—sizing up exits, calculating trajectories, identifying weak links—fired on all cylinders. The Traditionalists, swathed in tailcoats and moth-eaten disdain, had instantly formed a defensive phalanx around the more important members of their cohort. They moved as if allergic to both progress and polyester. The Modernisers had, in predictable fashion, gone feral. Phones out, some livestreaming the massacre with cheery commentary, others already editing the carnage into thirty-second highlight reels.

A footman in what must have once been bespoke livery but now qualified only as "tragic cosplay" staggered down the steps, hands clamped to his neck. Blood spurted between his fingers in time with the music still leaking from the auditorium. He tripped on a prone influencer and landed face-first at Vincent's boots.

Vincent bent down, gripped the man's chin, and exposed the wound: two neat punctures, ringed by bruises and the faintest dusting of powdered sugar. Lady Clore's work, then—she never did like to leave a scene without a signature garnish.

The dying man hissed out a final word—sounded like "cannelloni," but could have been "call an ambulance"—and expired, tongue lolling. Vincent stood, wiped his hand on the back of a Moderniser's hoodie, and called out: "Anyone got eyes on the source?"

Aurelia Voss, perched atop the balustrade like a Vanity Fair gargoyle, raised her hand and pointed. "Grand staircase. All the drama, all the time." Her ring light cast a halo over her platinum hair, catching every drop of blood in perfect detail for the feed.

Vincent nodded, then addressed his squad in the tone of a

man instructing a kindergarten on proper grenade etiquette. "Traditionalists: up the left flank, keep it tight. Modernisers: you're with me. Phones down, teeth out. If it tweets, bite it."

Cass Roe whooped, but the rest needed no encouragement. The team surged up the steps, Vincent at the tip of the wedge. Crystal flutes whistled down like ice daggers, some shattering on the stone, others splashing poisoned champagne into the mouths of the newly dead. Every so often, a flute would veer off, guided by unseen hands, and score a direct hit to the eye socket or exposed throat of an unlucky patron.

A bottle-blonde in an evening gown shrieked as she caught a flute in the hairline, then tumbled backwards, tearing down three others with her. A Moderniser caught the whole collapse on video and, without missing a beat, tagged it #BrutalBubbles before vaulting over the corpses.

Halfway up, Vincent's foot slipped on a pool of something viscous. He steadied himself, only to have a champagne flute spear the shoulder of his jacket, missing actual skin by a margin that would have impressed any phlebotomist. He yanked it out, sniffed, and grimaced. "Clore's got the cellar on tap. She's aiming for spectacle over efficiency."

Aurelia, beside him, smiled with approval. "Drama's the brand, darling. The more bystanders, the better."

Vincent grunted. "Then let's not disappoint her."

They reached the landing and spread out, the Modernisers already vining themselves into position behind ornamental pillars, the Traditionalists lurching forward with the determination of men who'd rather die than be caught running. Across the upper foyer, Lady Clore awaited, her silhouette backlit by the chandeliers, the lace of her dress dark as arterial spray.

She surveyed the carnage with a predator's serenity, then raised her glass. "Vincent Lupo. I was beginning to think the Council had gone vegan."

Vincent bared his teeth in a parody of a bow. "I'd say you look well, Euphemia, but the last time I saw that dress it was on a corpse."

Clore's laughter was a whipcrack, slicing through the babble of panic below. "You always were charming. Did you bring your own audience, or are these the Council's latest attempt at relevance?"

Aurelia answered for him, turning her phone screen to Clore with a dazzling smile. "We're trending, actually. You should check the numbers."

Clore regarded her with the patience of a spider evaluating a fly's résumé. "The world changes, but you don't, Vincent. Still hiding behind louder mouths."

Vincent advanced, flexing his hands. "I prefer to think of it as strategic delegation. You, on the other hand, haven't updated your playbook since the Crimean War."

Clore's eyes narrowed. She flicked her wrist, and three more flutes spun from the silver tray at her side. One missed entirely, pinging off the balustrade; the second caught a Moderniser in the thigh, who yelped, limped in a circle, then went back to filming; the third headed straight for Vincent's face.

He snatched it from the air, regarded the golden liquid, and —because the alternative was to show fear—downed the contents in a single swallow. For a second, nothing. Then his veins went to ice, and he doubled over, retching champagne and bile onto the landing.

Clore crowed. "Still the same idiot, too."

Vincent spat, wiped his mouth, and grinned. "Every time I think I've hit rock bottom, the nineteenth century hands me a shovel."

Behind him, the squads were making progress. The Modernisers had mapped the upper level, posting "live" updates to a network of followers who, astonishingly, believed every second. The Traditionalists had barricaded the side corridor, their leader—some Viscount whose name Vincent always forgot—now wielding a broken banister rail as if it were a holy relic.

Cass and Ren flanked Clore, keeping her penned on the upper landing. She watched them with disdain, her fingers caressing the crystal decanter at her elbow.

"Such a shame, Vincent. You could have ruled this city. Instead, you're a glorified event planner, cleaning up after bigger messes than yourself."

Vincent felt the poison fade, replaced by a surge of bloody-minded energy. "You know what they say: those who can, do. Those who can't, moderate."

He signalled to the Modernisers, who launched a barrage of flashbulb pops and blinding phone LEDs. Clore recoiled, throwing up an arm to shield her eyes, and Vincent lunged. He caught her by the wrist, twisted, and tried to wrest the decanter from her grip.

She was stronger than she looked. The two struggled, glass clinking between them, her fingernails biting deep into Vincent's hand. He could feel the venom working, but forced his muscles to obey.

"Let go, Euphemia," he growled.

She smiled, a slash of white in the gloom. "Make me."

Vincent head-butted her, once, hard. Bone connected with bone. For a moment, neither moved; then Clore staggered back, losing her grip on the decanter. It shattered, and the air filled with the choking sweetness of vintage death.

Clore backed away, clutching her ruined face. "You're not even Council anymore. Why do you care?"

Vincent wiped his brow, then gestured to the carnage below. "Because this city was mine before it was yours, and I'm not letting you rewrite the ending."

She sneered, then leapt for the balcony, her skirts billowing. Vincent lunged after her, caught only air and a flurry of black lace. Clore landed hard on a table below, scattering glass and limbs in every direction.

The Modernisers erupted in applause; a few even threw confetti. Vincent glared, then signalled the team to pursue.

He followed, three steps at a time, boots slick with the residue of spilled champagne and gore. As he reached the bottom, Clore was already at the far exit, leaving a trail of writhing bodies in her wake.

Vincent paused, panting, then looked back at his battered but intact squad. "Show's not over," he called. "If anyone wants a drink, now's the time."

Aurelia grinned, bloodied but radiant. "You really do know how to host a party."

Vincent smiled back, then led the pursuit into the night, the Royal Opera House echoing behind them with the screams of the poisoned, the click of cameras, and, faintly, the last notes of a dying aria.

The alley off Old Compton Street was the sort of back passage Soho did best: two bins per square metre, a puddle for every footstep, and the lingering aroma of ten thousand questionable nights. Ren sloshed through the first puddle, boots already caked in grime, and thought: at least it's not raining blood.

Yet.

At the alley's far end, a blue-white glow pulsed in time with a voice so hideous it made the neon seem tasteful. The crowd had formed in classic London style—spilling from the nearest bars, phones half-raised, some openly recording, others pretending not to. Every face was locked in the rictus of "I shouldn't be here but will definitely retell it tomorrow."

At the centre of it all, perched atop an old milk crate, was Algernon Bleak: the revenant poet, every cliché of the Victorian grotesque made flesh. His suit was the colour of surrender, his shirt a garden of mildew. The face was all cheekbones and wild hair, eyes glinting with the glee of a man who'd discovered new ways to ruin an evening.

Bleak declaimed at the night, each line of warped verse sending out a pressure wave that made the crowd flinch in involuntary synchrony. Every so often, a listener would fold to the ground, clutching their head and moaning, only to be replaced by another drawn in by the noise.

Ren braced herself against a wall, every muscle shrieking as the Mark on her arm lit up in time with Bleak's syllables. She gritted her teeth and hissed at Mrs Barley: "You sure you want to go first? I can take the bastard."

Mrs Barley didn't bother turning. "It's not a matter of want, dear. It's a matter of not having time to waste."

The next blast of poetry hit—a bastardised sonnet, all cheap rhyme and raw pain—and half the crowd doubled over. Ren felt it in her teeth, in her spine, in the marrow of her soul. The Mark throbbed so hard she thought it might pop straight off her skin.

Bleak saw them, and the smile went wider. "Ah, the audience arrives!" he bellowed, voice ringing over the huddle of the damned. "All the world's a stage, and tonight the players bleed!"

"Jesus Christ," muttered Ren. "He's doing the voices."

Mrs Barley, unflappable, marched right up to the milk crate and inspected Bleak from shoe-tip to hairline. "Mr Bleak," she said, voice even and dry, "this is not your venue. You are trespassing on a site of historical significance and causing a significant disturbance."

Bleak's laugh was a cough sharpened by a lifetime of regret. "Madam, I am the disturbance!"

He raised an arm, and the crowd's pain spiked. Ren's own vision doubled, then redoubled: every nerve ending, every memory, split and stuttered as if the alley itself were a bad signal. For a wild moment, she saw herself sprawled on the ground, fingers torn from clawing at her own ears, and knew it was only seconds before she joined them.

Mrs Barley didn't flinch. She circled Bleak, eyes on his hands, then his shoes, then the inside pocket of his ruined coat. "You're using old patterns," she said. "Clumsy, but effective. Did Ashcroft teach you that, or did you pick it up before the sanatorium?"

Bleak preened. "I have outlived all my teachers."

"Not your critics," said Mrs Barley, and jabbed him in the gut with her clipboard.

Bleak buckled, the wind knocked out. The poetry snapped off mid-couplet; the crowd shuddered and, as if a switch had been thrown, slumped to the ground or simply wandered away, suddenly more interested in kebabs or Instagram than the apocalypse.

Ren dragged herself upright, every joint fizzing with left-over agony. "Holy shit. You just... clocked him?"

Mrs Barley straightened her collar. "Never underestimate the power of correct form."

Bleak groaned, trying to suck air through his ruined lungs. "You can't stop the next verse," he rasped. "It's already written."

Mrs Barley knelt, folded up her clipboard, and slid it back into her bag. "Unfortunate for you, but I am the authority on site-specific hazards." She reached into Bleak's coat, fished out a sheaf of stained parchment, and tore it down the centre.

Bleak wailed, the sound far more human than any of his poems.

Mrs Barley stood, dusted her hands, and offered Bleak a polite nod. "Consider yourself redacted."

Ren pushed off the wall, shaking out her arms. The Mark dimmed, settling back to a dull ache. "He done?"

"For now," said Mrs Barley. "But the narrative's going to escalate."

Ren looked at the bodies littering the alley, then at Bleak, who whimpered like a child denied sweets. "Should I finish him?"

Mrs Barley shook her head. "No need. He's his own worst audience."

Ren laughed, even though it hurt. "We're up, then?"

"We're up," said Mrs Barley, already walking away.

The alley returned to normal: only the bin smell and the sticky footpath remained. Ren glanced back once, just to make sure Bleak didn't try anything, but he just sat there, cradling his torn papers and muttering fragments of verse to the indifferent dark.

"On to the next," said Ren, and followed Mrs Barley out into the wet Soho night.

Whitechapel, never a place for subtlety, had gone full apocalypse. The main drag was empty of civilians, the usual late-shift curry shops shuttered, but in the gutter between two mini-marts a war was under way. Baron Falkenhayn's contingent had arrived first, forming a human barricade along the curb. Each of his troopers stood braced, uniform immaculate even in the thick of blood and shattered glass, expressions set to "cold fury." Facing them, a mob of revenants in tattered Edwardian eveningwear, all teeth and malice, laid into the defensive line with antique canes, brass-knuckled gloves, and the occasional splintered bottle.

The French, never ones to miss an entrance, swept in from the north end, led by the Marquis Deveraux. His blade caught the streetlight and every neon shimmer from the nearby kebab shop, so that every lunge left a brief afterimage—a duel in negative, violence rendered beautiful for an instant before the spray of arterial black reasserted reality.

The battle's centrepiece was an overturned Uber, its driver still inside, screaming into his phone while the doors were battered by a ring of revenants in formalwear. "Help! Help! They are eating each other!" he yelled, as if customer service had a protocol for supernatural drive-bys.

Falkenhayn bellowed, and his line surged. The Germans advanced in perfect lockstep, canes glancing off the locked arms, then returning with the force of steel-tipped battering rams. The first revenant to break the line went down under three boots and a sabre thrust. The next two lasted longer, but the result was inevitable: in thirty seconds, the kerb was slick with ichor, and the Uber's windshield starred with the force of bodies hitting it.

Deveraux's squad did not so much fight as perform. They danced through the chaos, each cut and parry punctuated by a snide remark or a burst of laughter. One of his lieutenants beheaded a revenant with a slash of his sabre, then immediately toasted the corpse with a flask from his breast pocket. "To progress!" he declared, and the rest of the squad joined the cheer even as the carnage mounted.

Falkenhayn and Deveraux locked eyes over the heap of the dead, and for a second, old hatred outshone the mutual threat. "This is your fault," spat Falkenhayn, jabbing a gloved finger at the Frenchman.

"You wish you had such flair, *mon cher*," replied Deveraux, slicing a revenant's hand clean off and kicking the remainder into the path of an oncoming scooter. The scooter toppled, its rider leaping clear, and the revenant's head crunched under the rear wheel with a sound like a dropped melon.

A new wave of Victorian nightmares surged from a side

street, each armed with an increasingly ludicrous antique. One swung a fencing foil, another brandished a ceremonial mace, a third wielded an entire grandfather clock, using the swinging pendulum as a bludgeon. The clock face shattered against the back of a German's helmet, who shrugged off the debris and stabbed his attacker through the eye.

Deveraux raised his cane and parried the mace with effortless disdain. "You see, Baron? They have more imagination in their pinkie than your whole army."

Falkenhayn grunted, sweeping his adversaries aside with a disciplined efficiency that bordered on artless. "Imagination is not the same as victory, Marquis. You may wish to remember that."

They moved together now, each squad fighting back-to-back, old rivalries put on hold by the imperative of not being torn to pieces by the undead dregs of empire. All around, the city's leftover detritus became both weapon and terrain: scooters upended as tripwires, wheelie bins launched as projectiles, advertising posters flapping with each rush of displaced air.

Someone—possibly a revenant, possibly a bored bystander—lobbed a "Get Home Safe" sign like a discus. It caught Deveraux across the chest, knocking him into a lamppost. He rebounded, used the momentum to drive his sabre through the ribcage of the nearest foe, and came up smiling. "Ah, the public service of this city is second to none."

The last revenant, a skeletal thing in a blood-soaked cravat, made a break for the Uber, perhaps thinking to finish off the driver. Falkenhayn barked an order, and two Germans tackled the thing to the ground, holding it there while a third stomped on its skull until it split open with a hollow clunk.

Silence, for the first time all night. The only sounds were the whimpering Uber driver and the hiss of gas lamps burning off the city's last pretence at respectability.

Deveraux straightened, dusted off his ruined frock coat, and eyed Falkenhayn. "A pleasure, as always."

The Baron nodded, chin high. "May the best enemy win, Marquis."

They shook hands—brief, brutal, and instantly forgotten. Their squads fell in behind, each battered and bloodied, but upright.

Behind them, the heap of revenant bodies twitched once or twice, then lay still.

Falkenhayn turned to his men, voice like a funeral bell. "We move out. The next front will not be so easy."

Deveraux wiped his blade on a handkerchief, then produced another for Falkenhayn, who took it with a snort of derision. "For when you weep, Baron."

"Never," said Falkenhayn, but the edge had gone from his voice.

The two squads disappeared into opposite ends of the street, uniforms now indistinguishable from the city's dark. The Uber driver watched them go, then opened the door and crawled out of the wreckage.

# ELEVEN

After Whitechapel, Ren's flat felt less like a headquarters and more like an accident site with better snacks. Ren perched at the battered kitchen table, which groaned under the weight of blood bags (half-drained, some with polite straws sticking out), used bandages, and a slalom of instant noodle pots crusted with the residue of deadlines long missed. Every surface not already claimed by urgent paperwork or medical triage had been colonised by Zara's hoarder museum of the arcane: mismatched mugs filled with occult paraphernalia, commemorative ashtrays from vampire conventions, a jar of holy water (labelled "for emergencies only") next to a box of paracetamol.

Vincent slouched by the fridge, a stitched-up gash running from his collarbone to the crook of his left arm. He pressed a cold pack to the wound with the grim determination of a man who would rather bleed out than admit discomfort. A bottle of whisky, two-thirds murdered, stood at his elbow, as if offering legal counsel to the injured.

Mrs Barley, unbloodied but with her hair coming down in strategic wisps, attended to the worst of the casualties. She had arrayed the wounded like chess pieces around the kitchen: Ren, centre stage; Vincent, one square removed; and the rest of their battered team along the perimeter, each clutching their own assortment of wounds, painkillers, and existential regret. Occasionally, Mrs Barley muttered observations into her ever-present notebook, jotting each in a shorthand that no living soul could decrypt.

Ren kept her left sleeve rolled up. The Mark was in a petulant mood—throbbing blue and white, sometimes pulsing so hard it set her teeth on edge. She'd started the evening strong, mocking the Modernisers for their "post-battle selfie culture," but now her arm shook with a tremor that had nothing to do with adrenaline.

Vincent eyed her from across the room, his expression stuck somewhere between concern and 'I'd rather eat glass.' "That thing's got more personality than half the Council," he said, nodding at her forearm.

Ren snorted, then immediately winced. "Don't. Feels like it's trying to punch out of my skin."

"Let's keep the Mark in the room and not on the walls," Mrs Barley advised, voice as dry as a sherry trifle. She flicked her gaze over the others. "Everyone else holding up?"

A few muttered affirmatives, but mostly there was the dull thud of boots being unlaced, wounds being prodded, and a Moderniser in the corner trying to update his followers while pretending not to cry.

The Mark chose that exact moment to escalate. It brightened to a white-blue so pure it cast moving shadows against the kitchen ceiling, then sent a fresh bolt of pain from Ren's wrist to her shoulder. The surface of her skin shivered, then spidered with the first trace of ink-black cracks, radiating outwards like a time-lapse of a city falling into sinkholes.

Ren gasped, clutching her arm. The world telescoped, then slammed back into focus: the noise of traffic outside, the metallic clank of Mrs Barley's pen, Vincent's voice shouting her name.

She couldn't move her hand. The cracks were spreading, thin as spider silk but branching in every direction. They weren't just on the surface—they burrowed down, into the bone, carrying with them the cold certainty of something irreversible.

"Shit," she said, which about covered it.

Vincent was beside her before she even registered the movement. He caught her by the shoulders, steadying her as her vision doubled and her breath caught in her chest. "Oi! Ren. Look at me."

She tried. It was like trying to see through frosted glass, everything fuzzy at the edges. There were voices in her head— not whispers, not even proper words, just fragments and orders, half-sentences elbowing one another for room. She gritted her teeth, and a line of blood appeared between her lips.

"Stay with me, kid," Vincent barked. "Don't you dare let a bloody draft overwrite you."

The Mark pulsed again, harder. She nearly blacked out. Somewhere in the fog, she heard Mrs Barley mutter, "Clear the table," and in seconds the debris was swept to the floor, blood bags and paperwork and all, as Mrs Barley made space for whatever came next.

Vincent half-lifted, half-dragged Ren onto the table. He

leaned in, nose to nose, his own injuries forgotten, and patted her cheek with a shaking hand. "Snap out of it, Ren. You're not a prophecy. You're a stubborn little shit, and you don't get to die before I do, understand?"

She wanted to say something biting, something that would make him laugh or at least roll his eyes. Instead, her teeth chattered, and the Mark lit up so fiercely it left afterimages across the walls. The cracks snaked up to her elbow, then down, carving sharp black paths under the skin. It was agony and not, somehow—every nerve ending firing, but the pain swallowed up by the tide of sensation flooding her head.

Then came the voices: dozens, maybe hundreds, all speaking at once, a choir of the deranged and the doomed. She felt herself splitting, like a book with every page torn out and pasted onto a wall. Names, dates, fragments of prophecy—so much detail she could taste the ink.

She arched, gasped, and for a second Vincent looked genuinely frightened.

"Mrs Barley, she's—" he started.

"Hold her steady," Mrs Barley snapped, already pulling something from her bag—a strip of cloth, a fistful of smelling salts, a fountain pen.

Ren tried to speak, but her jaw wouldn't work. Instead, her arm wrote its own message across the table, the black lines gathering at her wrist and forming a new sigil in the wood: a spiral, then a set of runes, then a cross-hatch of tiny, perfect squares. The surface smoked, just for a second, and the whole kitchen filled with the smell of burnt sugar and ozone.

Mrs Barley held the salts under Ren's nose; the world cleared, briefly, and she managed to croak, "That... normal?"

Mrs Barley shrugged. "You're the first case I've seen, dear. But I have to say, you're setting the standard."

Vincent eased her back down onto the table, his arms still around her. "Breathe. You're alright."

She wanted to believe him, but the Mark throbbed again, and she knew—absolutely, in the part of her brain that had always run the numbers on every crisis—that she wasn't. The cracks weren't going away. They'd set in, like ink stains on cheap paper. She could feel the pull now, the Draft Eternal reaching for her, using her like a wick in a time-bomb.

She met Vincent's eyes, and for the first time saw fear there —not for himself, but for her.

"Sorry," she said, with a smile that felt like it belonged to someone else. "Guess I'm still the canary."

He pulled her close, silent for once. The whole flat went quiet, as if even the ghosts were holding their breath.

The Mark pulsed once more—an aftershock, not as bright as before but deeper, more final. It left her arm mottled with black, the sigil now etched permanently in the skin, a warning and a curse both.

Mrs Barley set down the notebook, fingers trembling just a little. "We'll need to act soon," she said, to no one in particular. "Next time, she might not come back."

Ren closed her eyes and let Vincent hold her, the smell of whisky and blood strangely comforting. She listened to her own pulse, to the silence in the flat, and to the not-so-distant sound of something scratching at the edge of her mind, waiting for the next crack to open.

The only thing scarier than losing herself to the story was knowing it might already have happened.

She hoped someone was keeping minutes.

After the crisis, Ren's world went very small: a tabletop horizon, Vincent's arm cradling her head, and the Mark—a burning brand that faded only as she lay absolutely, pointedly still. The rest of the room drifted in and out, first as a haze of panic, then as a grid of worried faces, each one orbiting her like moons around a dying planet.

It took her a full minute to notice Zara's ghost.

Where before Zara had drifted, blue and unfocused, this time she crackled into view with the intensity of a neon sign switched on in broad daylight. Every contour was hyperreal: cheekbones carved from clouded glass, hair floating and settling as if underwater, the thin line of her mouth set for once in something other than bemusement. She hovered not beside the table, but over it, suspended inches above Ren's arm. The air where she passed felt colder, like the inside of a butcher's fridge, and every time she shifted, her outline sizzled against the room's already-overloaded lighting.

Ren felt the weight of the attention and tried to lift her arm, but it wouldn't obey. She could feel Zara's gaze trace the cracks, mapping every jagged fork and vein. It didn't hurt—yet. But she knew, with a sinking, documentary certainty, that it would.

Zara said nothing for a long moment. She just watched the Mark, lips pursed in calculation, hands folded behind her back like a detective at a murder scene.

Mrs Barley broke the silence. "Diagnosis?" Her voice was

still clipped, but there was a tremor now, like a violin string stretched too tight.

Zara exhaled—a feat for the dead—and leaned closer, her spectral hands hovering just above the ruined skin. "It's not just acting up," she said. "The Draft Eternal is feeding through her. It's tethered to the Mark—she's the live wire."

Vincent bristled, his hands gripping the edge of the table. "Can you cut it off? Take the Mark, or block it?"

Zara's face didn't move, but her voice did: hard, brittle. "It doesn't work like that. Every time Ashcroft raises one of his revenants, it draws more power through her. Like with Carmine's prophecy, it's using her as a relay—every spell, every re-write, gets piped in through that." She nodded at Ren's arm, now a network of black filaments.

"So," Mrs Barley prompted, already taking notes. "Our options?"

Zara hesitated, and that was new. Usually, she had a list of solutions—improbable, distasteful, occasionally illegal, but always ready to hand. This time, she just floated there, mouthing silent calculations, until finally she said, "You stop Ashcroft, or you sever the chain. There isn't a third way."

Vincent's jaw clenched so hard the stubble whitened at the edges. "And if we don't?"

Zara met his eyes, her own hollow and merciless. "She gets overwritten. Erased. No afterlife, no legacy, just... gone. The Draft's last edit."

Ren felt all their stares turn her way. She let them have the silence, then forced a grin. "Guess that makes me the world's most inconvenient bookmark."

Zara almost smiled, but it was gone in an instant. "More like the first line in a chain letter. If you let this keep up, you'll infect everyone who's ever cared about you."

Ren wanted to snap back, but the quip hung in her mouth, dried out by terror. She looked at Vincent, hoping for a joke, a sneer, some shred of the old indestructible bastard. Instead, he looked ruined, his eyes wide and dark, every vein around the iris showing clear and black as calligraphy. His grip tightened on her wrist, gentle but final, as if he could keep her anchored just by refusing to let go.

Mrs Barley tapped the pen, then clicked it shut. "We need a plan," she said. "Now."

For a second, no one answered. Even the Modernisers—one with a bloodstained hoodie over his eyes, the other pretending to nap—had the decency to keep quiet.

Outside, traffic sounds filtered through the ancient glass, a tide of honking, shouting, and the distant threat of yet another siren. The world was moving on, as if nothing inside this flat could possibly matter. Ren felt the cold spread up her arm, the cracks settling in, and knew what the silence meant.

She was already halfway gone.

Vincent reached up, brushing the hair from her face. "We're not losing you," he said, voice soft as a funeral. "Not to him. Not to any of them."

She believed him—wanted to, at least. But the Mark pulsed again, and for a second she tasted ink and the dry bite of unfinished sentences. She shivered.

Zara receded, her outline flickering at the edges. "I'll monitor from the other side," she said. "If it escalates, I'll know."

Mrs Barley stood, already drafting orders. "We'll hit

Ashcroft before he can bring any more over." She eyed Vincent. "We need the city's best field agent. And a miracle."

Vincent gave a wry, broken laugh. "I'll get you one, but the miracle's on you."

Ren closed her eyes, listening to the hum of city and ghost alike, and let herself believe, for a moment, that they could pull it off. Or at least go down together, which was as good as family ever got.

The Mark, still warm, shuddered once more. She opened her eyes, stared at the map of black on her skin, and waited for the story to turn.

# TWELVE

Vincent sat slumped in the least offensive chair Ren's flat had to offer. It was upholstered in some oil-stained tapestry, the pattern only visible where decades of arse-polish hadn't worn it away. The room stank of death and disinfectant. Also: microwave ramen, printer toner, and, faintly, the scorched-ozone tang of London sunrise when it had the nerve to get in.

Thin daylight wormed around the edges of the curtain, slicing the flat into warring zones of blue shadow and pallid gold. Vincent's head lolled to the side, just far enough for a stray sunbeam to graze the back of his hand. It started as a pink flush, then a puckered white blister rose in the shape of a cat's paw. He hissed, yanked his hand back, and glared at the window like it had insulted his mother.

Ren, who'd curled herself into a ball on the sofa opposite, caught the movement. Her eyes, bloodshot and a bit wild, flicked from the blister to Vincent's face and back. "You know you could just close the curtains properly," she said.

He looked at the window again. A beam of light had moved, creeping along the floorboards toward his ankle. He considered moving his foot, then decided to see if the light would blink first.

The flat was a hoarder's paradise. Every available shelf, windowsill, and patch of wall was stacked with occult volumes, relics from Zara's years as an archivist, and the sort of knickknacks you only ever saw in jumble sales or murder-suicide estates. A trio of stuffed owls glared from above the television, a clutch of antique syringes sat in a pint glass by the sink, and beneath the table, a salt circle had been scuffed through by careless foot traffic. It probably didn't work anyway, but Vincent found its slow destruction comforting.

There was a commotion in the hallway. Mrs Barley, her hair rolled up in a state of permanent readiness, entered with a plastic bag clutched tight in both hands. She deposited it on the table with the gentle reverence of someone presenting an organ for transplant.

"Breakfast," she said, and peeled back the plastic to reveal a blood bag, hospital-issue, marked O-negative. A sticky red line had already seeped into the label, smudging the donor's name into anonymity.

Vincent's throat closed around nothing. He tried to muster a joke about the catering, but the hunger blanked everything else. He snatched the bag, tore it open with his teeth, and gulped the contents in three desperate swallows. It tasted like pennies and hospital corridors. He managed not to suck the bag flat, but the damage was done; blood had streaked down his chin, dotted the front of his shirt, and left his hands a sticky, surgical red.

Ren stared at him, her face a lesson in ambiguity—somewhere

between worry and disgust, with a side order of I'm-not-surprised-really. She tugged her sleeve down over her Mark, but not before Vincent caught the faint, blue-white pulse under the skin.

He licked his lips, wiped his chin with the back of his hand, and found he was shaking. He clamped down on the tremor, jaw rigid. "What?"

She looked away, so pointedly it hurt. "Nothing."

"Don't look at me like that. You don't get it."

Ren's gaze snapped back. "You think you're the only one losing control? My arm's turning into a bloody virus—if I sneeze, will the building catch it?"

Mrs Barley cleared her throat, loud and dry as parchment. "If either of you feels the urge to murder the other, do it in the bath. I just cleaned the carpets."

Vincent snorted. Ren made a noise like she might laugh, then didn't.

A draught—real or metaphorical—rippled through the flat. It caught at the curtain, lifting it just enough for a shaft of sun to paint Vincent's face in sickly yellow. This time, he didn't flinch, just stared it down, waiting for the skin to bubble. It did, slowly, tiny beads of water pooling on his cheekbone.

He closed his eyes, counted to ten, and when he opened them, Zara's ghost hovered over the far side of the kitchen. She was barely solid in daylight—just a suggestion of cheekbones and wild hair, her features smeared like a half-developed photo. She didn't say anything, but her gaze was on Vincent's hands, then on Ren's arm, then back again.

He wiped his mouth. "You enjoying the show?"

Zara's form fuzzed at the edges. "You're both falling apart

faster than the Council. At least they made it to the end of the century before imploding."

Mrs Barley busied herself with a mop and bucket, as if hygiene could restore order to any of this. "It's temporary," she said, but even she didn't sound convinced.

Vincent pushed himself upright, chair screeching across the floor. He staggered to the sink, found a glass, and filled it with water that tasted of ancient plumbing. He sipped, swirled, and spat red into the basin.

He looked monstrous. Felt it too. He wondered if that was the point.

Behind him, Ren pulled her knees up to her chest and pressed her sleeve tighter over her Mark. A fortune cookie, untouched on the kitchen counter from someone's takeaway order, seemed to glimmer with perverse optimism.

Vincent set the glass down and turned, catching Mrs Barley's eyes as she wiped the table free of blood. Her face was inscrutable, but the set of her jaw told him everything. She was ready to take his head off if it came to that. He wondered if she'd do it gently.

The silence returned, but this time it felt like the calm before an avalanche.

Vincent looked at Ren. "We need to end this," he said, and his voice sounded strange—like he'd borrowed it from someone less sure of themselves.

Ren nodded, just once. "Before it ends us," she said.

Zara's ghost drifted closer, her form resolving a little in the patchy light. "You might want to hurry," she said. "Ashcroft's not the patient type."

Vincent glared at the window, at the band of sunlight still

inching closer to his foot. He let it touch him, just for a second, felt the sizzle, the threat of erasure. Then he stepped back into the shadow.

He had the uncomfortable sensation that he was running out of places to hide.

The Mark on Ren's arm pulsed once, bright enough to throw new shadows on the ceiling. Vincent wondered, for a moment, if it was calling to him, or just keeping score.

Either way, the flat felt smaller by the second.

The city never shut up after midnight, but it did get weirdly specific. Out here, the air clung to the pavement with a wet, sour tang, as if all the failed nights of the week had been wrung out and left to fester. Streetlights flickered in sync with the dodgy transformer two blocks away, and every car that rolled past seemed to drag a fresh line of last orders and broken glass behind it.

Vincent walked ahead, hands jammed deep in his jacket, shoulders hunched. His whole body itched with the urge to be somewhere, anywhere, else. Ren trailed a few steps back, hoodie up, eyes alert but glazed—the look of someone doing hard maths just to stay upright. Zara floated along the gutter line, barely visible unless you caught her in the flash from a speeding cab.

Their mission was simple: patrol the streets, watch for anything that looked like a story trying to write itself into the fabric of London. Keep the Moderniser and Traditionalist squads from annihilating each other before the next Council summit. Try not to die in the process.

Vincent didn't care much for the odds.

They cut through the side roads toward the river, avoiding the main streets where the tourists still clustered. In the distance, a siren started up, wailing its way through Vauxhall, then faded. Zara's voice, calm and silvery, drifted out from the darkness: "Someone's raised a revenant at the Albert Embankment. Moderniser signature—probably a prank."

Vincent grunted, not slowing. "Let them handle their own mess. We're not babysitters."

Ren said nothing, just kept pace, her footsteps light on the broken paving. After a while, she murmured, "What's the point of these patrols, anyway? Ashcroft's not going to start the end of the world with a bunch of teenagers on ketamine."

Vincent half-turned, lips curled in a sneer. "It's not Ashcroft I'm worried about. The world ends one bad decision at a time."

They passed a kebab shop, still open, the bored counter guy watching TV behind thick glass. A drunk in an England shirt staggered by, clutching a bottle of Fanta and muttering something about Arsenal. The Mark on Ren's arm glimmered, every so often sparking brighter when the city's neon caught it just so.

They turned onto Lambeth Road. Somewhere ahead, the sharp report of shattering glass split the air, followed by the gutbucket roar of a crowd gone savage. Vincent felt the vibration before he heard the words: a pub brawl, big and messy, bleeding out onto the pavement.

Zara drifted ahead, materialising under the sign of The Anchor and Crown. She nodded at the chaos: "Ten on the street, two down already. One's got a knife. Police are a minute out."

Vincent swore. "We go in, we get filmed. You want to be viral again?"

Ren's face was hard to read, but she flexed her hand, knuckles whitening. "If we don't, someone actually dies. Isn't that the bit we're supposed to care about?"

Vincent hated that she was right. He hated it more when they crossed the street and the smell hit him: fresh, mortal blood, hot and wild and drowning out every other sense. The world snapped into high definition, every heartbeat within fifty metres telegraphing itself through his skull. He could hear the metallic rattle of the knife, the thick, ragged breaths of the wounded, the slick whisper of blood on tile.

His fangs extended before he knew it. He shoved his hands in his pockets, squeezing his fists so tight the nails bit flesh.

Ren spotted it. "You alright?"

"Peachy," he snarled, but his voice came out a register too low, too guttural. He could feel the hunger building, curling up inside him like a ball of razor wire.

He tried to steady himself, but the crowd surged, a body went down hard on the kerb, bleeding out, and the scent tripled in intensity. Vincent staggered, caught the railing for balance, and nearly tore it off the wall. He saw, in a haze, the brawlers shoving and spitting and laughing, even as the man in the cheap suit bled out into the gutter.

He couldn't breathe. He didn't want to. He wanted to feed.

He tore away from the railing, stumbling into a side alley, the world spinning as every instinct screamed to turn and bite, to tear out throats and bathe in the arterial spray. His vision narrowed to a pinhole, the edges ragged and black. He slammed his head against the wall once, twice, three times, hoping the pain would short-circuit whatever was happening inside him.

It didn't.

He slumped against the bricks, hands shaking, the taste of blood—someone else's, his own, he couldn't tell—flooding his mouth.

Ren followed, soft steps echoing in the narrow space. She stopped just out of arm's reach, arms folded, the Mark on her forearm glowing faintly under the streetlight. She didn't say anything for a long time.

Vincent tried to laugh, but it came out as a ragged cough. "Go on. Tell me I'm a fuck-up."

Ren's voice was quiet. "You're slipping. Pretending you're not won't save anyone."

He glared at her, but his eyes wouldn't focus. "You want to know what it's like? It's like drowning, except you want it. Every cell in your body wants it. You think I'm scared of Ashcroft? I'm scared of me."

She stared at the ground. "Join the club."

Vincent pressed his forehead to the bricks, the cold doing nothing to clear his head. He scraped at the wall with his fingernails, peeling off the paint. He felt his control slipping, and he didn't want to pull it back.

He said, "You should run."

Ren stepped closer, just enough for the light to catch her face. She looked tired, old in a way Vincent recognised. "If I run, I just end up here again."

Zara drifted into the alley, her glow barely illuminating the bin bags and discarded syringes. "For someone who hates being a vampire," she said, "you're doing an excellent impression of one."

Vincent ignored her. He slammed his fist into the bricks, hard enough that the skin split and blood oozed down his wrist. The pain was grounding, just enough to let him regain his breath.

He looked at his hand, the blood seeping from the knuckles. It wasn't enough.

The Mark on Ren's arm pulsed in time with his heartbeat, the blue glow flaring brighter with every throb. She watched him, and he watched her, and for a moment, Vincent thought he saw himself reflected in her eyes—not the monster, but the man who'd tried so long to pretend otherwise.

He sagged, breath hitching. "I don't want to go full Ashcroft. Not now."

Ren let her arm drop to her side. "Then don't."

He clenched his hand until the blood stopped. The air in the alley stilled, the sounds from the street fading into memory.

Zara hovered above the bin, her expression unreadable. "You can't outrun the ending, Vincent. You can only rewrite it."

He bared his teeth, not at her, not at anyone, just at the world in general. "Easy for you. You're already dead."

Ren shrugged. "We all are. You just get more chances to mess it up."

He tried to smile, but it didn't stick.

The city carried on. A police car whooped past, lights painting the alley in brief, garish flashes. Somewhere, another fight started up, or maybe it was the same one, echoing down the night like a bad habit.

Vincent stared at his bloodied hand, the skin already knitting itself back together, and wondered how many times he'd have to break himself before he stopped wanting to.

The Mark on Ren's arm faded to a low, steady glow. She said nothing, just watched, waiting for him to finish.

He flexed his hand, wiped it on his jeans, and straightened. "Let's go," he said.

Ren fell in beside him, silent. Zara shimmered, then vanished.

They walked out of the alley and back into the mess of the city, no better for it but, for the moment, still moving.

# THIRTEEN

No one had told the Houses of Parliament that the world was ending, so the lights still burned on the river and the clockface of Big Ben glared down with all the passive-aggressive insistence of a pub landlord announcing last orders. Westminster Bridge, never a safe place for existential contemplation, had become the precise moment where every dark and desperate part of London converged, like a badly-tuned orchestra still determined to outplay the apocalypse.

Vincent led the coalition through the freezing mist, head ducked against the wind, arms folded across his chest in a posture that was one-third insouciance and two-thirds trying to keep the sensation of his ribs from actively separating. He was followed, in no discernible order, by the rest of the city's finest: Ren, face set with the sort of stubbornness you only got from terminal denial; Mrs Barley, umbrella raised with the brisk efficiency of a staff sergeant on parade; and the ragged detachment of allies assembled through the world's most bloodthirsty WhatsApp group.

Behind them, the Modernisers walked in a wedge: Aurelia Voss at the tip, ring light in one hand and phone in the other, the blaze of her platinum hair throwing highlights on the council-provided ponchos of her followers. Cass Roe, flanking her, wore two phones and a GoPro, while Nyx Calder trailed slightly behind, sound deck strapped to his chest and fingers endlessly flicking at invisible crossfades.

On the opposite side marched the Traditionalists, led by a mortician's model of an elder in a frock coat that had outlived three monarchs. Each of his deputies wore a powdered wig, which would have looked ridiculous if not for the way their faces had been stripped of anything resembling humour or hope. Their presence drew a clear line down the centre of the coalition, which no one crossed except to spit, glare, or in one memorable case, attempt to trip a Moderniser with a walking cane.

The German and French delegations brought up the rear, the former in tight, ironed formation, boots rising and falling in rhythm, every face set to the expression "I would rather die than admit this is undignified." The French had gone for the opposite approach, smoking, bickering, and occasionally whacking each other with gloves for imagined slights. If anyone in the crowd had managed to forget the last century of international politics, these two contingents were here to ensure the memories remained at the surface, thrumming and bitter.

Vincent had no love for the city, or for Parliament in particular, but as they passed through the security cordon—now reduced to a single, shell-shocked special constable, who waved them through on the theory that anyone headed for Westminster at this hour probably had a better reason than his pay grade permitted—he felt a pang. Not nostalgia. Not even regret. Just the cold certainty that if you gave monsters a seat at the table, they would eat the chairs, the tablecloth, and possibly the table itself.

They reached the heavy, triple-locked doors of the Palace, and Mrs Barley gave the team a look that brooked no argument. "We proceed as planned," she said, voice like a whipcrack in a morgue. "No improvisation. No heroics. We get to the Chamber, secure the objective, and neutralise Ashcroft and his ilk with minimum narrative fallout. Is that clear?"

Vincent snorted. "Crystal. Unless anyone's expecting a plot twist."

Cass, already live-tweeting, raised a hand. "Plot twist is trending. Just saying."

Mrs Barley ignored him, squared her umbrella to the ready, and led the charge up the steps. The doors, either unlocked by design or forced open by an earlier, less subtle party, swung inward with a groan that echoed all the way to the Central Lobby.

The air inside was thick with the tang of burning paper and spilt ink, and something else—something sweeter, but with a metallic undertone that Vincent recognised immediately as the scent of the recently undead. The corridor was a massacre of tradition and taste: banners torn down and nailed back up at mad angles, statues of long-dead politicians daubed in lipstick and correction fluid, busts of statesmen wearing party hats and, in one case, a soiled nappy.

Ren muttered, "Is it just me, or does it smell like the set of a particularly bad panto in here?"

They pressed forward. The only sound was the distant, staccato thump of something—someone—banging a gavel with the force of a car crash.

Mrs Barley stopped them at the threshold of the Chamber. She pointed, wordless, and let the team take in the scene for themselves.

The House of Commons, already the most theatrical room in the country, had been transformed into an abattoir of ceremonial dignity. The green leather benches were stained black with blood-ink, some of it still glistening in the overheads. Every seat was filled—not with MPs, but with Ashcroft's revenants, each one tailored to the theme: Victorian grandees in shredded court dress, spinsters with bonnets veiled in cobweb, a few actual children in sailor suits who hissed and clawed at each other like kittens dipped in napalm.

At the far end, the Speaker's chair was occupied by a skeleton in morning coat and sash, its empty sockets fixed on the floor as it pounded the desk with an ivory gavel. Every strike sent a ripple through the benches: the revenant MPs would rise, shriek their "Ayes" or "Nays," and then collapse back into their seats, sometimes leaving behind pieces of themselves as they did so.

On the floor, two revenants squared off in what could only be described as a ritualised slap fight, overseen by a revenant in a judge's wig and another holding an actual hourglass. The subject of debate was unclear, but judging from the state of the "loser" (now missing half his scalp and most of his left arm), the House had come down in favour of violence.

Vincent heard the proposals before he could see the source: a chorus of twisted, plummy voices rising and falling in half-baked Latin and mangled parliamentary jargon.

"Mr Speaker, I move that the next Order of Business be the public flagellation of all traitors to the Draft!"

"Seconded, with an amendment—let the flagellation commence on the hour and be livestreamed to every seat in the nation!"

"Objection! The honourable member for Kensington is not yet sufficiently reanimated to enjoy the proceedings!"

"Point of order: the member is a fraud and a corpse!"

Every word was a parody of governance, and Vincent felt the icy hand of memory slip down his spine. He'd seen this before—once, in the Black Death, when the city had surrendered to its own funeral. Once, in the Blitz, when the air raid wardens outnumbered the living. Now again, as the city wrote its own obituary in real time, one joke at a time.

The coalition advanced, first in stealth, then in force. The Modernisers split off, Cass and Nyx heading for the press gallery, Aurelia leading her camera crew down the aisle with the poise of a catwalk model at a wake. The Traditionalists fanned out in a pincer, the leader brandishing a silver-topped cane and a roll of parchment that, if Vincent had to guess, was probably a list of eligible successors in case the current lot didn't survive.

Mrs Barley waved Vincent and Ren toward the central table —the site of so many bad decisions in the city's history, it was a wonder the wood hadn't fossilised from shame.

Vincent paused, took in the madness, then nodded to Ren. "Democracy was already a farce," he said. "Now it's just better dressed."

She grinned, the Mark on her arm pulsing with anticipation. "Think anyone will notice if we steal the mace?"

"Only if you tweet it," he said, and led the way.

As they advanced, the German and French contingents clustered behind them, both sets of eyes fixed on the carnage with the hungry fascination of bystanders at a motorway pileup. The Germans muttered among themselves, their language a machine gun of contempt and precision, while the French delegation compared the current spectacle unfavourably to "that unfortunate episode in the National Assembly," though none could agree which year they meant.

Two of the Modernisers took up positions near the Serjeant at Arms, who was now a stitched-together thing with a pike and the clear intent to use it. They livestreamed every moment, Aurelia narrating in the tone of a lifestyle vlogger discovering that her subscription box contained a severed finger. "We are here, darlings, in the actual seat of power, and let me tell you: it is an experience. Hashtag VampireParliament is trending."

Cass, never content to follow, snaked around the benches, popping up every so often with new, increasingly bizarre selfies. Nyx provided the musical backdrop, layering the shrieks and moans with basslines that rattled the remaining windows.

At the table, Vincent found himself facing the revenant Speaker, who had given up on the gavel and was now hurling handfuls of paper at the air, each sheet covered in blots of black script and what looked like the occasional human tooth. "Order!" it screeched, "Order! The House will come to order, or the House will burn!"

Ren, unfazed, leaned over the rail and said, "Isn't it supposed to be the Order Paper?"

The Speaker's jaw clattered, then fell off entirely, dropping to the floor with a neat click.

Vincent turned to Mrs Barley. "That's our cue."

She nodded, drew the umbrella close to her chest, and motioned for the rest of the coalition to converge.

The German and French squads, hating each other only slightly more than the revenants, staged a joint assault down the centre aisle. The Germans moved like a wall, shields up, canes brandished like riot batons. The French swept in from the side, swords drawn, their leader shouting *"Pour la République!"* as he vaulted a bench and drove his blade through the midsection of a revenant in full livery.

The Traditionalists followed, a flotilla of lace, brocade, and powdered rage. Each one brandished something silver or wooden or, in one case, a crucifix the size of a rugby ball.

The Modernisers, meanwhile, kept up a running commentary, phones held aloft, ring lights blazing.

The Chamber descended into chaos. Revenants leapt from the benches, some hissing, others mewling, a few reciting fragments of old Hansard as they bled ink onto the carpet. Every blow from the coalition sent up a spray of something—blood, or ink, or the fine white dust of ancient bones.

Vincent waded in, fists and fangs and every last reserve of rage. He saw Mrs Barley drop three revenants in a row, the tip of her umbrella puncturing sternum and skull with surgical precision. He saw Ren, arm lit with the Mark, rip a revenant from the throat with a single, brutal twist. He saw the Modernisers—Aurelia in particular—duck and weave through the carnage, never missing a shot, never missing a beat.

He saw, above it all, Zara's ghost flickering in and out of the public gallery, her face tight with anxiety, her hands conducting the battle as if it were an orchestra that could still be saved from collapse.

He saw Ashcroft.

At the centre of the Chamber, where the blood pooled deepest and the noise was a living thing, Ashcroft waited, hands folded on the table, watching the spectacle with a smile that suggested he had been born to rule the end of things.

"Mr Lupo," he called, voice rising above the slaughter. "So nice of you to bring guests. I hope you don't mind, but we've restructured the order of business."

Vincent bared his teeth. "You're all out of tricks, Ashcroft. Even this isn't original."

Ashcroft spread his hands, mock-modest. "Nothing is original, Mr Lupo. We're all just drafts, waiting for someone better to edit us. The only question is who gets to hold the pen."

Vincent lunged, fangs extended, but Ashcroft was faster, sidestepping with a grace that made a lie of his death. They clashed, and for a moment it was just the two of them, surrounded by the fury and the rot, fighting over the only prize left: who got to decide what happened next.

Around them, the coalition drove the revenants back, seat by seat, bench by bench. The Germans, battered but unbroken, locked arms and pushed a wedge up the centre, their leader shouting orders in a voice that made even the dead flinch. The French, bloody and laughing, whirled their swords and cut through anything that moved.

Vincent and Ashcroft grappled at the edge of the table, hands locked, fangs inches from each other's throats.

Ashcroft smiled. "This is the future, Mr Lupo. You can fight it, but it will consume you."

Vincent leaned in, voice low and ragged. "Only if I let it."

With a surge, he broke the grip, drove Ashcroft back, and flung him over the table.

The Speaker's chair did not so much explode as fragment, the upper third launching into the air with the force of a grenade. Ashcroft hit the carpet in a tangle of antique upholstery and hubris, and Vincent leapt the table after him, boots squelching in a slurry of blood, ink, and shredded blue books. Around them, the chamber had devolved into a single, heaving scrum: coalition vamps and revenants locked in mortal (or at least narratively final) combat, the odd Moderniser ducking out from under a brawl to snap a selfie before diving back in.

Vincent's landing was ugly but effective—he drove his knee into Ashcroft's chest and his fist into Ashcroft's face, the latter making a noise somewhere between a coconut and a cathedral bell. For one sweet second, he thought he'd broken the bastard's jaw. Instead, Ashcroft spat out a wedge of tongue, then grinned, a mess of blood and teeth knitting itself back together as Vincent watched.

"Predictable," Ashcroft sighed, as if disappointed. Then he twisted, using the torque to catch Vincent behind the knee and flip him flat. Vincent landed hard, arms flailing for purchase, but Ashcroft was already up, silhouette backlit by a cascade of glass as the Speaker's gavel soared overhead and embedded itself in a chandelier.

Ashcroft brandished a walking cane—ostentatiously Victorian, all silver filigree and malice. He lunged, bringing the tip down in a whistling arc, and Vincent rolled just enough to avoid losing an ear. The cane split the flagstones where his head had been, chips flying. Vincent swept a leg, but Ashcroft danced clear, his feet moving in precise, duellist's steps—half sabre, half ballet, all ego.

Elsewhere on the chamber floor, Ren and Mrs Barley had cornered their own problem: Lady Euphemia Clore, the poison socialite was also in attendance. She lounged atop the government bench, twirling a jewelled fan whose every flick spattered the air with a fine mist of black fluid. "Honestly, girls," she drawled, "I thought we'd agreed on a ceasefire for fashion emergencies?"

Mrs Barley answered with the umbrella, spinning it so a burst of buckshot silvered the air in a cone. The fan absorbed most of it, but a few pellets grazed Clore's shoulder; where they hit, the skin sizzled and smoked, releasing an aroma like burnt treacle. Clore pouted. "So uncivilised."

Ren, flanking left, drew a kitchen knife and swung with a ferocity that would have bisected any normal skull. Clore anticipated—she always did, in life or after—and bent double at the waist, the blade scything only a lock of hair and part of the bench's inlay. She sprang at Ren, hands stretched like claws, and this time her words were the real attack.

"Little mouse!" she spat, the syllables hot and laced with supernatural venom. They landed on Ren's cheek like boiling water, and she yelped, falling back with a hand to her face.

Clore advanced, voice rising: "You don't belong here. You're nothing! Not Council, not prophecy, just a footnote—"

Mrs Barley cut in, umbrella swinging, and the two locked in a standoff of cane versus fan. The impact set up a ripple in the air, and for a moment the pressure in the chamber dropped, like the room was gasping for breath. Ren, half-blinded, scrambled behind the clerk's table, pulling the knife out of the upholstery with one hand.

Mrs Barley pressed the attack: "You've always been an ornament, Euphemia. No substance."

Clore laughed, and the sound was poison, too. "At least I'm remembered," she said, and with a snap of her fan sent a jet of venom across Mrs Barley's face. Mrs Barley got the umbrella up, but some of it splattered her wrist, and she hissed as the skin blistered beneath the glove.

Ren, teeth clenched, holding the knife by its blade, steadied her aim from the crook of the table. "You want your cameo, Clore? Smile." She threw the knife. It spun, blade over hilt, and caught Clore just below the eye, and the revenant dropped, body twitching in a puddle of her own toxic runoff.

Above, Aurelia Voss sprinted along the press gallery, the halo of her ring light painting every drop of violence in cinematic definition.

The judge's revenant launched itself, gnashing, but she sidestepped with the smoothness of a cat and jammed her selfie stick into its open mouth. The phone's flash went off, point-blank. The revenant staggered, howling, and tumbled backwards off the rail, shattering a lamp on its way down. Aurelia dusted her hands, adjusted her hair, and turned the camera on herself: "We now return you to the action."

Cass Roe, meanwhile, had decided that the benches were parkour terrain. He bounced from seat to seat, dodging flying daggers and the less metaphorical flying limbs of the combatants. "This is monetisable!" he shouted, voice rising above the carnage. "I'm gonna have sponsorships for days!" A razor-edged ballot box whistled past his ear, nicking the tip and drawing a perfect bead of blood. Cass howled, then filmed his own wound. "Exclusive content, motherfuckers!"

Nyx Calder, his DJ decks now fully weaponised, crouched behind the ruined Speaker's dais. His hands moved in impossible patterns, and with each pass a fresh sub-bass wave rippled out, knocking incoming revenants off their feet and sending them tumbling into the melee below. "Beat drop in three... two..." he intoned, and on the count, unleashed a pulse so deep the entire Commons vibrated. Revenants staggered, their eyes rolling, and several simply collapsed as the sound liquefied whatever passed for their brains.

Vincent, for his part, had no time for spectacle. Ashcroft came at him with a flurry of cane strikes, each one a lesson in how much pain could be inflicted with the right leverage and the complete absence of empathy. The cane raked his thigh, slammed into his ribs, then—when Vincent parried with an improvised mace made from the Speaker's jawbone and spinal column—swept low and took out his ankle.

Vincent went down, breath forced out in a sharp hiss. Ashcroft stood over him, immaculate even now, the cane's silver head dripping red. "You never had vision, Lupo," he sighed. "Always clinging to old stories, never brave enough to write your own."

Vincent glared, blood pooling in his mouth. "You never wrote a word in your life. You're just a footnote with ideas above your station."

Ashcroft bared his teeth. "Maybe. But I'll be the last footnote that matters."

He swung the cane for Vincent's temple, but Vincent

caught the shaft and bit down, fangs shearing through the wood. He spat the splinters into Ashcroft's eye, then lunged, jaws wide. Ashcroft countered, and the two locked up, their faces inches apart, each trying to force the other into submission by the simple expedient of biting off the other's head.

It was stalemate, in the worst sense—neither could get the angle, both were losing blood, and every second spent locked up was another second for the chaos to close in.

Around them, the battle reached its fever pitch. The Germans, battered but operational, had formed a wedge, their leader now armed with a broken flagpole and a fistful of sharpened iron crosses. The French had staged a dramatic last stand on the opposition benches, Deveraux at the centre, fencing three revenants at once while his lieutenants lobbed champagne bottles as improvised grenades. Every so often, a bottle would explode, spraying a revenant with a cocktail of fizz and powdered silver. The affected undead shrieked, then combusted in a pillar of blue flame.

Traditionalists and Modernisers, natural enemies, now fought in tandem: one running interference, the other blinding and tripping the foe, both gleefully ignoring the bad blood in the pursuit of not being eaten alive by the past.

At the edges of the room, Zara's ghost wove in and out of the gallery, her form flickering and distorting as if the battle was overloading even the spirit realm. She drifted through the walls, eyes locked on the centre, mouthing words Vincent couldn't quite hear.

Ashcroft, furious now, broke the lock and kicked Vincent square in the chest. Vincent slid backwards, landing among the ruins of the dispatch box. His vision swam; he heard, more than saw, Ashcroft advancing.

Ren, seeing Vincent down, recovered her knife and threw it in Ashcroft's direction. It was on target, but Ashcroft was simply too fast, and he sidestepped. It punched a hole through Ashcroft's shoulder, spinning him half around. He roared, not in pain, but in the outrage of being interrupted.

"Pissant!" Ashcroft howled, and before Ren could move out of the way, he was on her, hand locked around her wrist. The Mark on her arm flared, burning hot enough to ignite the air. Ashcroft recoiled, hissing, but did not let go.

Vincent struggled to his feet, every part of him screaming. He grabbed the nearest weapon—a broken fragment of the ceremonial Mace, still humming with old magic—and charged.

He didn't shout, didn't banter, just drove the Mace head into the back of Ashcroft's skull with every ounce of weight and momentum he had left.

The blow staggered Ashcroft, but did not fell him. Instead, he turned, one eye gone black and leaking ink, and smiled. "You're so predictable, Vincent. Always thinking you can win by committee."

Vincent spat blood and swung again. This time, Ashcroft caught the Mace in one hand, wrenched it free, and brought the shaft up in an uppercut that caught Vincent under the jaw and nearly severed his head. Vincent dropped, blind and deaf, the world reduced to a cold blur. He felt the boot coming for his chest, but there was nothing he could do.

It never landed.

Instead, there was a shriek—a sound so high and fierce it left afterimages in the air—and suddenly Ashcroft was the one being driven backwards, a slim black shape clinging to his face. It was Nyx Calder, who'd abandoned the turntables in favour of a more direct intervention. He'd wrapped a length of speaker wire around Ashcroft's neck and was tightening with all the conviction of a man who'd never paid a TV licence in his life.

Ashcroft thrashed, hands clawing at Nyx's arms, but the wire only bit deeper. Then, with a final twist, Nyx yanked Ashcroft off his feet and sent him crashing through a stained-glass window, the fragments tumbling after him in a glittering rain.

Vincent, barely conscious, watched as Ashcroft disappeared into the night. He tried to move, but every limb felt remote, like someone else's failing machinery. He heard, distantly, the cheer as the coalition realised Ashcroft was gone.

He tried to smile, but the effort cost too much.

Mrs Barley was at his side a moment later, propping him upright, her own face streaked with burns and blood. "We did it," she said, voice flat from exhaustion. "He's gone."

Vincent shook his head, or thought he did. "Not gone," he mumbled. "Just... moved on to the next draft."

Ren, face half-burned and beautiful with it, limped over and knelt beside him. "You alright?"

Vincent managed, "Never better." Then he coughed, the red spray catching the light, and added, "I give it five minutes before the next story starts."

Cass Roe, now bleeding from three different places, took a group selfie with the battered survivors. "Can I get a quote for the socials?" he asked, phone poised. "Hashtag: the future?"

Aurelia, never one to be upstaged, popped into the frame,

flashing her best smile. "Hashtag: 'We Came, We Saw, We Got The Stains Out.' Now trending in twelve countries."

Nyx, bruised but grinning, slumped down next to Vincent. "Was that punk enough for you, old man?"

Vincent almost laughed, but the sound got stuck halfway. "Could've used more bass," he said, and meant it.

The chamber, ruined but for the moment secure, buzzed with the afterglow of survival. Revenant corpses melted into pools of narrative runoff, the worst of the damage already fading as the city's immune system did its slow, impossible work.

Above, Zara's ghost hovered in the shattered gallery, her outline flickering with a kind of urgency. She gestured for the survivors' attention, and when the last of them looked up, she said:

"Every spectacle feeds the Draft Eternal. Every audience makes it stronger. Don't get comfortable—this was just the dress rehearsal."

Vincent, head swimming, locked eyes with her. "What's the encore?"

Zara's smile was thin as a knife. "The next one writes itself."

The warning hung in the air, colder than any grave.

And for the first time in centuries, Vincent Lupo hoped like hell he wouldn't be around to see the final act.

# FOURTEEN

The walk from Parliament into the street should have been a victory march—flags, confetti, a cake with Ashcroft's face carved into the icing. Instead, it felt like the coda to a particularly vicious funeral: silence punctuated by coughing, the shuffling of too many boots, and the slow seep of blood from wounds that refused to close.

The survivors—the ones who still had their original limbs and enough ego to walk upright—limped down a side street off Whitehall, led by Mrs Barley's umbrella and the promise of an unbuggered exit. The night was cold and damp, the sort of air that turned even the freshest kill into a flavourless porridge. A few humans and late-shift taxi drivers paused to stare at the procession, then hurried on, driven by a shared intuition that nothing in this alley was worth the risk of a second look.

Vincent trailed near the back, boots squelching in what he hoped was just rainwater, though the colour was wrong. Modernisers hunched, swiping away at their phones with blood-stained thumbs, already composing narratives of heroism and minimal actual damage. The Traditionalists walked as if still in session, heads high, hands clutching the wounds in their sides like a point of honour. Behind them, the Germans and French lagged a pace or two, as if the fight was ongoing and anyone caught in the middle might be shot for desertion.

He counted the casualties. Nyx was missing a tooth, but wore the gap with pride, grinning at every passing car as if daring them to ask. Aurelia had a gash on her cheek—just under the makeup, almost artful—and was using it as leverage for sympathy from her followers, who dutifully filmed her best angles and ignored the swelling. Cass had bandaged his arm with a strip of neon scarf, but the blood had already saturated the fabric, leaving a trail of red on the pavement. The rest were as battered as pride allowed, every one of them glancing back at the Houses of Parliament as if afraid it might sprout legs and chase them down.

Vincent wiped at his jaw, smearing revenant ichor into his stubble, and scanned the huddle for Ren. For a wild moment, he thought she'd been erased in the fracas, collateral damage to one of Ashcroft's rewrites. Then he caught sight of her at the edge of the group, standing apart, eyes fixed on nothing, sleeve pulled down as if trying to hide her arm from herself.

He veered off, ignoring the side-eye from the Moderniser with the camera, and closed the gap in three long strides. The Mark had always been a showy bastard, but tonight it was trying for a world record: the blue-white radiance pulsed through the threadbare cotton, painting Ren's hand in ghostly shadow. Her face was pale—not just the regular pallor of someone who'd lost too much blood and too many arguments, but the washed-out tone of an object left too long in the sun, colours draining out second by second.

"Hey," he said, stopping just out of reach. "That thing lighting up for Christmas, or have you got plans I should know about?"

Ren didn't answer. She didn't even blink. The only sign she'd heard him at all was a tiny quiver in her fingers, a twitch that rippled down to the tips and set the air around her hand fizzing. The Mark was burning her, that much was obvious, but the way she held her arm—tight to her chest, like a bomb about to detonate—suggested it was doing more than just surface damage.

He stepped in, closer, caught her scent. He knew she was afraid. Her lips parted, but the words stuck, like they'd forgotten how to arrange themselves.

Then her knees buckled.

It wasn't a graceful collapse; it was as if someone had yanked the bones out of her legs and left her to drop, lifeless as a spent match. Vincent lunged, caught her by the waist just before her skull hit the cobblestones. She weighed next to noth-ing. Less than nothing. The pressure of her body in his arms was so slight he had the mad thought she might float away if he let go.

"Ren!" he barked, his voice too loud in the empty street. Her eyes fluttered, not quite opening, not quite shut. She was shaking, but not from cold.

The nearest vampires paused, circled in, faces scrubbed raw by the night's events. None dared get closer. Vincent cradled Ren's head, brushing hair from her face, and stared helplessly as the Mark flared brighter, now blinding, etching the bones of her hand in negative. "Shit. Shit. Someone—Mrs Barley! Get over here!"

Mrs Barley, who had just finished negotiating a truce between two Traditionalists and a Moderniser, broke from the pack and hustled over. The umbrella was gone; the usual steel-boned calm replaced by something closer to honest panic.

She knelt beside Vincent, her voice clipped but shaking at the edges. "Let her down. Flat. Easy now." She took Ren's wrist, thumb pressed to the pulse point, and frowned at what she found—or didn't.

Vincent lowered Ren to the pavement, careful as if setting down a loaded trap. "She just dropped. One minute she's there, the next—" He bit off the rest. The truth was, he'd seen this before, or something like it, when Zara's ghost had glitched out during the showdown with Bartholemew and the Cloaked Lady at the Orpheum theatre. He did not want to see what happened to a human brain that tried to handle it alive.

Mrs Barley peeled back the sleeve, exposing the Mark in all its glory. The blue-white sigil throbbed, veins beneath it now webbed with black, the tendrils climbing up Ren's forearm in frantic scribbles. For a moment, Vincent was sure he saw movement under the skin—tiny, branching lines crawling toward her shoulder, her neck, her face.

Mrs Barley hissed through her teeth, then looked up at Vincent. "She's being rewritten," she said, as if naming the thing might slow it. "If it succeeds—"

"—she's gone," Vincent finished, anger souring his voice. "Properly gone. No ghost, no afterlife. Nothing."

Mrs Barley nodded, her jaw clenched so tight he could hear the grind of molars.

The Mark pulsed again. Ren's eyes snapped open, but it wasn't her looking out. For a second, the irises glowed with the same sickly blue as the sigil, and her lips moved in sync with a voice that was both hers and entirely other. When she spoke, it came out as a choir, one register above and one below her natural pitch, the words overlapping like a haunted voicemail.

"The vessel empties," she whispered, "the mask falls—" Her body arched, then convulsed once, hard enough to knock Mrs Barley's hand aside. "All stories end."

Then she went limp. The light drained from her arm, the Mark settling to a dull, ugly grey. Her breathing was shallow, barely there.

Vincent stared, feeling the bottom drop out of his insides. He cradled her, hands shaking, blood smeared on his palms and hers. For once, the sarcasm failed him. All he could do was hold on, and hope the story hadn't finished with her just yet.

For a long minute, the alley held its breath. Even the Modernisers' phones fell quiet, their feeds frozen mid-upload, the audience—worldwide, for all Vincent knew—captivated by a slow-motion disaster. The only movement was the twitch of a muscle in Ren's jaw, and the way the Mark on her arm crawled, fractal and relentless, toward her heart.

Then the temperature dropped. Not the usual, "someone left the fridge open" chill, but a sharp, localised cold that made Vincent's scalp tighten and his gums itch. He looked up, expecting another batch of revenants or, worse, a Council clean-up team with more sense than scruple.

Instead, Zara's ghost materialised at the edge of the circle. She was less substantial than ever, her outline flickering as if the rules of solidity had gone on strike. The blue-white of her spectral form was dull, almost translucent, edges bleeding into the smog. She moved with the slow focus of a diver under pressure, each step a negotiation between this world and the next.

She knelt beside Ren, her hands hovering inches above the Mark. "Don't touch her," said Mrs Barley, but the warning was reflex only; Zara couldn't touch anything anymore, not even the living.

Zara studied Ren's arm with the clinical detachment of someone who had autopsied their own corpse. The cracks had spread past the elbow now, veins blackening as the sigil drank whatever passed for Ren's life force. With each pulse, the darkness leached further, up the shoulder, across the collarbone, and out along the jawline.

The air was a meat locker, and Ren was the only fresh cut. With every beat of the Mark, her colour faded—black webbing across the skin, blue flashes in the eye, each movement less human, more a piece of grim statuary inching toward completion. Zara's ghost drifted closer, hunkered down beside the broken body, and studied it with the precision of a mortician called in for a botched exorcism.

She said nothing for a long moment, just stared. Mrs Barley hovered at her back, fists balled in a way that suggested she was one bad result away from putting the whole team out of its misery. Vincent, not trusting his voice, watched as the cracks began to reach Ren's lips, splitting them into a red-raw geometry.

It was Zara who spoke first, her tone flat as a death certificate: "It's burning through her. The Draft's not just using her—it's feeding on her. Every new revenant, every rewrite Ashcroft made, ran through this." She tapped the Mark, or tried; her finger passed straight through, flickering as it went.

Mrs Barley's jaw flexed. "Can it be reversed?"

Zara looked up, eyes glassy. "No. Not from here."

Ren shuddered, breath coming short and tight. A patch of blue-white flame danced along the veins in her neck, flared, then guttered. Her hands spasmed open, fingers splayed, and the cracks ran from nailbed to elbow.

Vincent went cold. He shifted Ren gently, resting her head on his knee. The ghost of a memory played out in his mind—another battlefield, another casualty, the exact same helplessness. He tried to think of anything to say, but the words had all been chewed to pulp by centuries of failure.

Zara's face softened, just a fraction. "She's not gone yet. But if the Draft isn't severed from her—now—she'll be overwritten. Not even a shadow left."

Vincent looked up, lips peeled back from his teeth. "And if we do break it?"

Mrs Barley's gaze was level, ancient. "We lose our only link to Ashcroft. The Draft goes fully autonomous, and we're blind."

Zara nodded, hunched in closer. "You have to end the link at the source. But it will kill her, or worse."

Ren spasmed, body arching. Vincent caught her, hands pressed to her shoulders. She was ice to the touch, flesh thinning to parchment. He tried to think of the right words, but nothing landed. All he could do was hold on.

Then, without warning, the scent hit him.

He'd smelled Ren a hundred times, a thousand—her sweat, her hair, the metallic tang of her blood after a fight. He'd always ignored it, trained himself to block it out, or at least pretend the urge was something else. But now, with her skin going transparent, with the veins thrumming right there under his hands, the hunger crashed in like a riot through a shopfront.

His fangs were out before he even noticed. The urge was so sharp, so sudden, he reeled, nearly dropped her. For a second, all he could see was the pulse at her throat—so weak, so easy, so close. His vision doubled, the world going pale at the edges, and he heard his own voice say "No" without meaning it.

He tore away, staggered to the far wall and pressed his forehead to the bricks, fighting the pull with everything left in him. Every muscle in his body wanted to turn back, to sink his teeth in, to end the ache, but he held. Barely.

Behind him, Mrs Barley's boots clicked on the cobblestones. She moved with the poise of a judge at sentencing, but there was no satisfaction in it. Just an old, tired sadness. She stepped between Vincent and Ren, faced him dead-on.

"You know what has to happen," she said, not a flicker in her voice.

Vincent bared his fangs, shook his head hard enough to rattle his skull. "No. There's another way."

Mrs Barley didn't blink. "There isn't. The Mark's an open conduit. If you don't take it out now, the Draft will use her to birth a new story. You know what that means."

He gripped the wall so hard his fingers left imprints. "She's not a battery. She's a person. She's—" He swallowed, coughed. "She's Ren."

Mrs Barley's mouth twisted, the closest she'd come to sympathy in months. "That's why it has to be you."

He shook his head again, but the logic was relentless. Only a predator could cleanly end a thing like this—no spell, no rite, just teeth and blood and a mercy sharp enough to beat the Draft at its own game.

He slid down the wall, landing in a heap. His hands shook, nails gouging at the mortar. "I can't."

Mrs Barley looked at Zara, whose form was barely holding together, patches of her face blinking in and out with every other breath. "She can't hold much longer," she said. "If you don't do it, the Draft will finish the job."

Vincent stared at the cobbles, at his own battered boots, at the fragility of Ren's outstretched hand. He wanted to say something heroic, or defiant, or even just coherent. All he managed was: "I won't damn her. Not after everything."

Mrs Barley crouched, voice gentle. "She's already damned, Vincent. This is the only thing left. Come on, it's now or never. We'll take her to the crypt."

# FIFTEEN

The crypt under Westminster was not on any public tour, for which even the dead were grateful. It had started as a Roman undercroft, picked up some Norman sensibilities, and now looked like the aftermath of a thousand-year drunken argument between church, state, and several generations of very angry masons.

Tonight, it was home to a collection of creatures who would have been ejected from any self-respecting haunting for lowering the tone.

Candlelight flickered across rows of stone columns, their surfaces scored with the graffiti of centuries: hearts, prayers, anatomically precise dicks. Wax drooled from wall sconces in mutant stalactites, puddling on the dirt floor where rats had thoughtfully chewed escape routes for the truly desperate. The survivors of the Parliament disaster had barricaded the entrances with old tomb slabs and the sort of fire doors only installed in British heritage sites after at least three actual fires.

At the crypt's heart, Ren lay on what could, with a generous interpretation, be called a bed: a plank, two bags of sand, and Vincent's jacket as a makeshift pillow. The rest of the coalition —what was left of it—clustered at a respectful but anxious radius, swapping injuries and side-eyes. No one was especially eager to get closer.

Vincent was the exception. He knelt beside Ren's pallet, arms wrapped tight across his chest, shoulders hunched as if preparing for a verdict he'd already memorised. His skin, paler than the stone behind him, twitched at every motion from the makeshift bed. He kept his eyes on her face, and nowhere else.

Ren had not moved for nearly ten minutes. Her breathing, barely audible, was so shallow it could have been mistaken for the crypt's background sigh of ancient rot. The Mark was back, bigger than ever: the blue-white sigil had turned the colour of bad ink, and its filaments snaked from her forearm to her throat, up into the veins beneath her jaw. A black stain spidered her neck, and every so often the veins would pulse, as if her body was in negotiation with itself about whether or not to carry on.

Mrs Barley stood nearby. She wore the same suit as always, though it now bore new battle scars—a tear at the shoulder, a dusting of Parliament ceiling in her hair. Her eyes moved from Ren to Vincent, then back, the calculation clear in the set of her jaw.

Above the scene, Zara's ghost flickered in and out of visibility like a cheap LED. Her face, never more than half-solid, had an edge tonight—her cheekbones sharper, the frown lines deeper, her eyes lit with the tired fury of someone watching their best work shredded and pulped for newsprint. Every so often she drifted lower, hands hovering over Ren's chest as if she could jump-start the heart by sheer proximity.

Ren's eyelids fluttered. She let out a noise: not a gasp, not a moan, just the dry, uncooperative cough of a person trying to surface from under eight feet of wet sand. Vincent startled, reaching instinctively for her hand but stopping just short, as if afraid to catch whatever new mutation the Mark had in mind.

Ren coughed again, and this time opened her eyes. The pupils were dilated, almost black. She took a slow inventory of the crypt, then focused, unblinking, on Vincent.

"Water," she croaked. The word sounded like an accusation.

Vincent fumbled with the flask at his belt, poured a measure into a cracked mug, and held it to her lips. She sipped, then turned her head away, staring at the stone ceiling.

Vincent watched her for a long, silent minute. Then, barely above a whisper: "I can't. Not to you. Not like this."

Ren flexed her fingers, found his sleeve, and pulled. For someone so nearly gone, her grip had the authority of a closing iron maiden.

"It's not damnation," she said, her voice steadier now. "It's survival. My choice. Do it."

Vincent shook his head. His hands shook too, even as he gripped his own knees so hard it left a line of bruises.

Mrs Barley stepped in, her voice matter-of-fact, as if she was reciting from a training manual: "She's given her consent. That makes it binding."

Zara's ghost hovered closer, eyes flicking from Mrs Barley to Vincent and back. "If you wait, she'll be gone before the ink dries," she said. Her voice had lost its wryness; it was urgent, brittle, and, for the first time, a little afraid.

Vincent looked down, then up, then away—anywhere but at Ren's arm, where the black veins now pulsed in time with a heartbeat that was rapidly losing the argument. He wiped his mouth with the back of his hand, then reached for her wrist.

Ren gripped his hand, nails digging crescent moons into his skin. "Do it," she said again, and the words were as close to gentle as she ever got.

For a moment, nothing moved except the drip of wax and the shifting light on the wall. Then Vincent's fangs, dormant for most of the night, extended of their own accord—a reflex, a betrayal, or maybe just a suggestion.

Vincent shook, whole body going numb. He looked at Ren, so pale now she was almost see-through, the Mark fading to a shadow on the skin, the cracks already knitting themselves into new, alien patterns.

He thought of the stories, of every time he'd failed to stop the ending, of every soul he'd watched get eaten by something bigger and colder than fate. He thought of Zara, half-gone; of Mrs Barley, stoic as ever; of Ren, who'd never asked for any of this and would probably mock the drama even as it erased her.

He looked up, caught Mrs Barley's eyes. She nodded, just once, and moved aside.

Vincent crawled to Ren's side. He brushed the hair from her face, wiped the blood from her lips. She wasn't quite gone—her chest rose and fell, barely, a breath per minute, maybe less. He pressed his forehead to hers, whispered something neither of them would remember.

Vincent hesitated, jaw set. "You sure?" he asked, the last lifeline.

Ren's laugh was just a thin exhale, the ghost of her old disdain. "I'd do it myself if I could reach."

Vincent nodded, once, and lowered his mouth to her throat. He bit.

The crypt filled with the smell of iron, salt, and something more ancient. Ren arched, then stilled, her fingers tightening on Vincent's hand until he thought they might snap bone. The blackness in her veins surged, then seemed to retreat, leaving her skin almost translucent.

Vincent drew, then stopped, pulling back as if burned. Blood—brighter than it had any right to be—ran down Ren's neck, then slowed, then stopped altogether. He wiped his mouth, looked at her face, and waited.

For a long moment, nothing. Then Ren's eyes rolled back, and her body went slack.

Vincent rocked back, cradling her head. He looked up at Mrs Barley, then Zara, then down at his hands, which were no longer shaking.

"Did I—?" he started, but the words were drowned by a new pulse from the Mark. The blackness receded, replaced by a steady blue-white glow.

Mrs Barley leaned in, pressed two fingers to Ren's throat. She waited, then nodded. "Still there," she said, as if logging a power outage.

Zara's ghost slumped, visible relief ghosting her features.

Vincent let out a breath he didn't remember holding.

He stroked Ren's hair back, just for a second, and whispered, "Sorry."

The crypt, silent as ever, offered no judgment.

But for the first time all night, the Mark seemed to rest.

After, the crypt was very quiet. Even the phones had stopped recording.

For a long time—seconds, maybe years—Vincent watched Ren not breathe. The world around them had muted itself to a pressure-cooker hush: the coalition frozen on the margins, the columns slicked with flickering candlelight, even the rats gone silent, as if awaiting instructions. Vincent's hands, still locked around Ren's head and wrist, found no pulse. He flexed his fingers, desperate for warmth, and felt only the faint suggestion of body heat draining into the flagstones.

There had been too many corpses in his history for Vincent to mistake what came next.

He'd meant to savour the moment, or at least to mark it with something resembling respect, but the act itself had been rushed, brutal, unceremonious: a punch-through-the-tissue bite, the bare minimum of restraint. Even now, the hunger churned beneath the nausea, the taste of Ren's blood—singular, sharp—etched on his tongue like battery acid. His body remembered it. So did his guilt.

He looked up at Mrs Barley, whose face had the pained blankness of a civil servant reading an obituary for a colleague she'd secretly despised. "Is she—?" Vincent started, but his voice snagged and quit.

Mrs Barley knelt, again she pressed two fingers to Ren's

throat, then shook her head. "She's gone," she said, voice both a verdict and a dare.

Zara's ghost, flickering above, exhaled a non-breath. "You did what you had to."

Vincent rocked back on his heels, hands still cradling Ren's jaw, knuckles white. He tried to let go, but his muscles wouldn't answer, so he just sat there, hunched, eyes shut, waiting for something—an aftershock, a protest, a sign of life.

Nothing.

Then, the sound: a ragged, monstrous inhalation that seemed to rattle the mortar from the walls. Ren's chest heaved, once, then again, as if she was learning oxygen from scratch. Her eyes shot open—no gentle fade, no Hollywood slow build—just blank darkness for a moment, then a red so pure it looked backlit by murder. She howled, an animal sound, and the whole crypt jumped as one.

Vincent scrambled to catch her, because she launched upright with the hydraulic force of a mousetrap, head snapping side to side, mouth open in a full, savage snarl. The new fangs were bigger than Vincent's, and sharper, the points catching the candlelight in a line of white that was almost comic in its intent.

Ren groped for his face, caught his collar, then shoved him away with a strength that made his spine pop. She tried to stand but hit the low ceiling at speed, bounced, then landed on all fours, teeth bared, every muscle twitching with the urge to fight or flee or feed.

For a second she didn't seem to know where she was. She hissed, lips peeled back to show every tooth, and blinked at Mrs Barley, then at Zara's ghost, then back to Vincent, who was already scrambling to intercept her next move.

"Ren," he said, as calmly as he could manage, "it's me."

She stared at him, every part of her vibrating. "I know," she said. Her voice was different, the vowels chewed raw, the consonants clipped short. She lurched forward, grabbed Vincent's sleeve, and pressed her face to his neck.

Vincent braced, waiting for the bite. Instead, Ren just inhaled, deep, a rolling tide of hunger. Her chest shuddered with the effort.

Mrs Barley edged closer, clipboard held up like a shield. "Ren. You're in transition. Can you understand me?"

Ren bared her fangs at Mrs Barley, who did not flinch. Then, slowly, Ren eased off Vincent's neck, licked the blood from her lips, and sat back on her heels. She blinked twice, the red fading from her eyes, then started to laugh—a thin, shattered giggle that sounded halfway between relief and brain damage.

"Shit," she managed, wiping her mouth with the back of her hand. "That's a rush."

Vincent hovered, hands out, ready to restrain or comfort or both. "You alright?"

Ren grinned, showing fangs. "You tell me. Are you still scared of me?"

Vincent, remembering the strength of her grip, thought about it. "Not scared. Just adjusting."

Ren flexed her fingers, marvelling at them as if they'd just been grafted on. She drew a slow line along her forearm, where the scar pulsed. But it wasn't black anymore: the tendrils had thinned to a filigree, red-purple, the energy channelled into a single, spiralling sigil just above her wrist. She tapped it, curious, and the scar pulsed in reply, humming under her skin.

Zara's ghost dropped lower, face twisted with a kind of joy

Vincent had never seen on her. "You did it, kid. You're still you."

Ren shot her a look. "Speak for yourself," she said. "I'm starving."

Mrs Barley relaxed, just a millimetre, and made a note. "Hunger is normal in the recently undead. We have provisions." She nodded at a battered cooler in the corner, then back to Vincent. "She'll need stabilising. And a mentor."

Vincent blinked, caught flat-footed. "Me?"

Mrs Barley nodded. "You made her. She's your responsibility."

He looked at Ren, who was now sitting cross-legged, eyes shut, hands folded as if in prayer. She seemed at peace, but Vincent could feel the heat radiating off her—an engine running at full tilt with nowhere to go.

He sat beside her. "You okay?"

Ren opened her eyes. The red was gone, replaced by the same dark brown as before, but brighter, sharper, almost alive. "Never better," she said. "What happens now?"

Vincent shrugged. "We figure it out. One hour at a time."

Zara's ghost hovered between them, her form stabilised, a faint smile ghosting her lips. "You broke the Draft," she said to Ren. "You're free."

Ren flexed her arm, watched the scar spiral, then smiled. "Guess the story isn't finished after all."

Vincent laughed, just once, and it was real.

The rest of the coalition, watching from the edge, slowly exhaled. One by one, they found seats on the nearest slab or box, the tension easing from the room.

Mrs Barley clicked her pen, satisfied. "Welcome to the next phase," she said. "Let's make sure it lasts."

In the cold, the candles guttered and wept, casting new shadows on old stone. For the first time in years, Vincent Lupo thought he might actually have something left to teach. Ren, for her part, looked hungry enough to devour the world.

It seemed a fair trade.

And somewhere, high above, London ticked on, blissfully ignorant that the end had been postponed for at least one more night.

# SIXTEEN

Ren paced between two ancient columns, ears ringing with every sound the world could possibly scrape together. The place was meant for the dead, but tonight it was all too alive: the shuffle of boots, the hiss of breath through split lips, the dull symphony of coalitions in crisis. Candles guttered along the walls, their flames jittering at every footfall as if terrified to commit to anything. In the far corner, a makeshift camp had been laid out for the battered survivors, most of whom looked ready to trade allegiances for a clean blanket and five minutes of silence.

Not that silence was ever going to happen. Ren's new ears picked up everything: the drip-drip-drip from some invisible leak high in the vaults, the papery rustle of Mrs Barley's clipboard, even the sharp, staccato pulse of Vincent's finger tapping the stone as he watched her from the far side of the chamber.

She flinched at every echo. A footstep thirty yards away crashed through her skull; a cough from the German contingent felt like a punch to the solar plexus. Even the candles seemed to mock her, each pop and sizzle amplified until she wanted to snuff them all, one by one, with her bare hands.

Worst of all was the scent. The mortals—the coalition foot soldiers, the field medics, the ones who'd survived Parliament with nothing but stitches and adrenaline—reeked of blood. It clung to their skin, oozed from their wounds, hung in the air like a sickly-sweet fog. She could count every injury in the crypt by smell alone, trace every droplet back to its trembling owner. The urge was worse than thirst, worse than hunger; it was a full-body revolt, every cell screaming at her to pounce, to tear, to feed.

She reeled, stumbling into a column for support. The cold shocked her palms, and she gripped the stone with white-knuckled intensity, nails digging half-moons into the ancient surface. Her body shuddered, not from cold or fear, but from the raw, untethered need to bite and drink and keep biting until nothing hurt anymore.

The scar on her forearm—her old Mark, the one that had tormented her for weeks—itched under her sleeve. It pulsed whenever she got too close to the humans, a warning or an invitation, she wasn't sure. She tried to ignore it, but the itch became a burn, then a throb, flaring with every beat. She found herself scratching at it, at first absent-minded, then with increasing ferocity, as if she could rip the craving out of her own skin.

Vincent drifted closer, boots soft on the flagstones. He kept a careful distance, like she was a bomb that might go off in any direction, but his eyes never left her. "You need to sit," he said. "It gets easier if you don't fight it."

Ren spat a laugh, though the sound came out jagged. "That supposed to be comforting?"

He shrugged. "Worked for me."

She pressed her forehead to the column, inhaled the mineral cold, tried to focus on the grit and lichen rather than the blood pooling in the corner. "I thought it'd feel different," she said, voice muffled against the stone.

Vincent crossed his arms, gaze still fixed. "It doesn't. Not for a while. You just learn to live with it."

She peeled herself from the column, swayed a little, then forced her legs to move. Every step sent a fresh jolt through her spine, as if the crypt itself was wired to her nervous system. "No," she said. "You learn to pretend. Whole world's run by people pretending they're not monsters."

He almost smiled, but caught himself. "That's the first lesson."

She bristled at the implied mentorship. "Don't start lecturing. I know what I am now."

He stepped in, just close enough to block her path, then held up his hands in peace. "I'm not judging," he said. "I'm warning. The hunger doesn't stop. You think you can fight it, but it'll win if you let it. You can't—"

Ren shoved past him, shoulders colliding. "I said stop."

She stumbled deeper into the crypt, only to be pinned by a half-dozen stares: coalition vampires, some eyeing her with predatory interest, others with the sort of bureaucratic anxiety that meant her file had already been started. On the bench nearest the wall, a Moderniser with a stitched scalp and two bandaged arms watched her like she was a cautionary tale in progress. Ren bared her fangs—automatic, not even meant to threaten—and the Moderniser blanched, gaze darting away.

The scent of his blood called her anyway. It was sharp and hot, edged with fear, and for a moment she wanted nothing more than to leap the bench and tear his throat open. The urge hit so hard she staggered, nearly fell, and had to grab the stone table to steady herself.

From the shadows, Zara's ghost wavered into being. She hovered just above the ground, face more solid than usual, her hair backlit in a sickly spectral corona. "Congratulations," she intoned, voice dry as old leaves. "The family's got a new vampire. And she's already moodier than you, Vincent."

Ren glared at the ghost. "You here to help or just haunt?"

Zara gave a one-shoulder shrug. "Depends. How many of these coalition types do you plan to maim tonight?"

Ren's jaw locked. "None," she said. "Not unless they get in the way."

Vincent, now at her shoulder, didn't hide his worry. "She means it," he said to Zara. "She's running hot."

Ren wheeled on him, hackles up. "I can speak for myself, thanks."

Zara flicked a finger at the scar on Ren's arm. "That's going to keep flaring up, you know. Every time you get hungry, it'll call louder."

Ren pulled her sleeve down, hiding the scar, but she couldn't block out the ache. She tried to move away, but every exit was blocked by more stone, more bodies, more blood.

She dropped to a crouch, arms wrapped tight around her knees, and rocked. The motion helped a little, but the noises wouldn't stop, the smells wouldn't stop, the itch under her skin grew until she was sure she'd claw herself to ribbons. She dug her nails into her thigh, tried to concentrate on pain that was hers, but it only made things worse.

She could feel Vincent's presence looming, his hunger harmonising with her own, a duet of need and restraint. She wanted to hate him for it—wanted to blame him for making her like this—but she couldn't. Not when every cell in her body was singing the same awful tune.

"Go away," she whispered, but even to her own ears it sounded weak.

Vincent sat on the floor beside her, cross-legged, arms on knees. He didn't speak, didn't reach out, just sat there, breathing in sync with her. The tension in his shoulders matched hers perfectly.

A beat passed. Then another.

Zara, satisfied with her entrance, drifted closer. "You could try biting him," she suggested. "It won't fix the cravings, but it might break the tension."

Ren managed a laugh, though it came out more like a snarl. "I'm not giving him the satisfaction."

Vincent snorted. "You couldn't take me if you tried."

She wanted to snap back, but the hunger was back in force, the itch in her arm a siren now. She squeezed her hands together, hard, until her knuckles shone through the skin.

"Just let me... deal with it," she said.

Vincent nodded, as if he'd expected nothing less. "I'll be here," he said, softer than before.

She curled tighter, head buried in her arms, and waited for the next wave to pass.

Around them, the crypt was silent for a few blessed

moments. Even the drip from the ceiling seemed to slow, as if the world itself was waiting to see who broke first.

Ren closed her eyes, focused on the hunger she felt. She could almost hear it whisper: this is the new story. This is how it goes.

She wasn't sure if it was a curse or a promise.

But she wasn't letting go.

There were corners in the crypt where even the bravest light failed. Vincent found one: a narrow alcove off the main vault, its entrance framed by the limp banners of forgotten rebellions, its floor bare but for the dust and the bones of abandoned construction. The air here was so cold it burned the lungs, and every word or footstep from the main chamber arrived muted and off-key, as if the world outside existed only in translation.

He paced the length of it, over and over, boots biting into the hard-packed dirt, jaw clenched so tight his teeth buzzed. He wanted to punch a wall, or scream, or both. Instead, he balled his fists and walked in short, brutal loops, muttering curses at the ground. When he stopped, it was to glare at the ceiling, willing it to collapse and end this string of stupid decisions before he made the next one.

He leaned his forehead to the chill of the stone, pressing so hard the skin went numb. The echo of Ren's voice—her last words, every snap and hiss—played through his head like a bad song on repeat. He'd meant to save her. He'd meant, for once in a long, long time, to do something right. Instead, he'd delivered her into a waking nightmare and had the gall to act like a mentor about it.

He was still there, eyes shut, when Mrs Barley slipped into the alcove. Her presence was as distinct as ever: no wasted motion, no pity in her eyes, clipboard held at parade rest. She paused just inside the gloom, then squared up to Vincent as if she was about to deliver bad news to a man who'd known nothing else.

"Brooding never fixed a thing," she said. "You should come back. She'll need help."

Vincent grunted, but didn't move. "She doesn't want my help. She wants me dead. She just hasn't worked out how to say it yet."

Mrs Barley's lips quirked in what might, under a microscope, be called a smile. "If she hated you, she'd already have tried. Newly turned are not known for their restraint."

He exhaled, the cold turning his breath to vapour. "I shouldn't have done it. Not to her. Not when she had a choice."

"She was out of choices," Mrs Barley said, voice flat. "You made a decision. She's alive because of you. Don't waste time regretting what's done."

He spun, hands outstretched in useless argument. "Alive is a technicality. She's one of us now—she'll never get back what she lost. You saw what it did to me. To all of us."

Mrs Barley closed the gap, set her clipboard on the ledge, and leaned in, all business. "It's not about you. She's stronger than you think. And you—" She jabbed a finger at his chest, "—are not the tragedy you want to be."

Vincent snorted. "Wouldn't bet the crypt on that."

Mrs Barley considered him, then turned to leave. "Self-pity

is boring," she said, her shoes clicking on the flagstone as she vanished back toward the main hall.

He watched her go, the rhythm of her steps fading into the shuffle of the larger world. He wanted to follow, but couldn't make his feet move. He wanted, for the first time in ages, to apologise to someone. Maybe even to Ren.

He sank to a crouch, one hand braced against the wall, and stayed there, waiting for the stones to answer.

At the top of the stairwell, Ren stood perfectly still, hidden by shadow and the ragged banner that hung like a warning above the alcove. She hadn't meant to eavesdrop, but every word had carried up the steps, clear as if Mrs Barley had whispered them in her ear. She'd heard everything: the anger, the guilt, the ache in Vincent's voice when he said her name.

She gripped the railing, knuckles gone white, scar pulsing in time with her own racing heart. It was a strange thing, listening to someone fall apart for your sake. Stranger still was the realisation that his fear—the fear of having ruined her, of being hated—was almost a perfect match for her own. She'd wanted to scream at him, to throw every accusation she could muster, but all she felt was the hollow space where rage should be.

She pressed her palm to the stone, feeling the way it absorbed heat and memory, the way it anchored her in place. She slid down the stairwell, knees drawn to her chest, and listened as Vincent's pacing began again. He moved like a caged thing, relentless, never letting himself rest.

She thought about what Zara had said: that the hunger never stopped, that you only learned to pretend. It sounded miserable, but it was also something Vincent had survived for centuries. If he could do it, so could she. Maybe.

She let her head fall back, eyes on the invisible ceiling, and whispered, "We're in this together now."

The words were barely audible, even to her own ears. But she felt the truth of them in her bones, in the scar's steady thrum, in the way the stone gave back nothing but acceptance.

She stayed there, listening to Vincent's circuits, until the sound became something like comfort.

They didn't have to be monsters alone.

Below, in the dark, Vincent finally stopped pacing. He stood, back pressed to the wall, and closed his eyes.

Above, in the stairwell, Ren matched him, shoulder to the cold and breathing slow.

Neither moved.

But for the first time since the crypt had closed around them, they both let themselves believe the night might end without disaster.

And for a moment, it was enough.

# SEVENTEEN

The hall at the Council of Pale Affairs—such as it was—had once hosted a centuries-old boys' club dedicated to "the preservation of the Empire and the ordering of its supernatural affairs." On a normal night it smelled of old wood polish, cheap tobacco, and the kind of English gin that could strip paint. Tonight, the air was seasoned with burnt paper, and the faintly metallic tang of battle sweat. The ancient oak tables had been muscled together in the centre of the chamber, their surfaces carpeted with maps, topographical overlays, and an unsteady procession of wax-dripping candles. Several of these burned with a blue flame, as if chemical fire might impress upon the assembled the seriousness of the occasion. It did not.

Baron Falkenhayn stood at the table's northern edge. His uniform—black, pressed, adorned with the subtlety of a brass band—was as unruffled as his manner, but the set of his jaw suggested that, given his preference, he would sooner be on the front than delivering a committee report. Behind him, the Germans stood at parade rest, each perfectly aligned by height and haircut. Their faces, even the recently dead ones, bore the rigid self-loathing of men who had seen too much and then been ordered to see more.

On the opposite side, the French contingent had attempted a visual counteroffensive, but the effect was more "Louis XVI's last stand at the barbers" than disciplined martial threat. Their leader—Marquis Deveraux, who had likely never attended a battle where the uniform code did not include lace—had managed to find a cape with actual bloodstains as accent, and wore it with a flourish that verged on necromantic. His lieutenants fanned out behind him, every lapel torn and every eye glinting with the acid glee of men planning a coup they could never actually finish.

Vincent Lupo watched from the darkest patch of shelving, next to a bookcase whose "restricted" section had been gutted for fuel. His injuries had sealed themselves up, but the swelling around his left eye had stuck around out of pure spite, a memento from Ashcroft's parting gift. He clutched a mug of something boiling and unpleasant, letting the steam fog his field of vision.

Mrs Barley, still immaculately pressed, hovered by the door with her clipboard. Every few minutes she made a note, her pen a silent metronome keeping time for the meeting's mounting absurdity. Ren, resplendent in her only other hoodie and an aura of near-terminal discomfort, sat on the bench closest to the radiator. She kept her eyes on her hands, which seemed to have acquired a tremor that only abated when she pressed her wrists to the scalding metal.

Falkenhayn's turn came first. He inclined his head with the precision of a man trained to treat even oxygen as a resource. "As of this morning, my contingent numbers thirty-six. Down from eighty-eight at assembly. All accounted for: seven total destroyed, eleven compromised, six missing in action—likely disposed of by Ashcroft's people. Twelve wounded but operational, the rest combat-ready." He rattled off the numbers like reading out scores at a particularly bleak sports day.

He finished with a click of the heels, then stood aside. The French, upstaged before their performance could begin, responded with a well-rehearsed Gallic sigh. Deveraux swept forward, a faint smear of blood beneath his chin not quite hidden by the powder.

"The French detachment," Deveraux began, "remains at thirty-one. We have sustained seven losses—two to the English, three to your Ashcroft, one to what I believe was a regrettable misunderstanding with the Soho constabulary, and one to despair, which I am told is a new record for this kind of gathering."

The room tried not to react, but a few snorts from the Moderniser table slipped through.

Deveraux gestured, magisterial. "Nevertheless, my officers and I remain committed to the defence of this city, however little the city seems to wish it. We are prepared to stand until all is lost, or until the Germans finish their war and require us to pick up the pieces as usual."

He punctuated the sentence with a bow, which might have been mocking or might have been a deeply held tic. The line between the two had been worn smooth by centuries of abuse.

A silence landed, heavy and awkward. Deveraux's men

straightened, chins lifted. Falkenhayn's jaw went even more rigid, if possible, and the faintest tremor ran through his right cheek.

Falkenhayn said, "We die for the same cause." The words might have been drawn from a manual, but they rang in the room with a sincerity that startled even the speaker. He nodded at Deveraux. Deveraux nodded back, solemnly, and for a moment the old hatreds curled up and took a nap.

Vincent, who could not bear the weight of uncut emotion even in a city as sarcastic as London, slouched further and muttered just loudly enough for the nearest three rows: "That's the most romantic thing I've heard all week. And I spent half of yesterday drinking with a Frenchman and an ex-priest."

Mrs Barley shot him a warning. Ren, who had not looked up once, winced visibly. Her new senses, Vincent guessed, registered the mutter as a klaxon.

Someone else spoke. "Order," said a woman at the head of the Traditionalist table, her face as sharp as the creases in her suit. "We have survivors on all fronts, but Ashcroft's forces will not be the last to test us. We must set the line of resistance tonight, or London will fall by morning."

A flurry of response followed—Modernisers yammering about digital strategy and optics, Germans requesting precise lines of attack, the French arguing for "flair" in the approach. Through it all, Vincent watched Ren: the way her hand trembled, the way her breath came in tight bursts, the way she blinked twice as often as anyone else in the room. He tried to catch her eye, but she was locked in a silent, private argument with her own biology.

He thought about standing, about saying something to calm

her or at least to shift the focus elsewhere. But he knew better. If anything could out-stubborn a newborn vampire, it was the Council's procedural inertia.

He settled for a smile that was more scar tissue than reassurance.

Mrs Barley, clipboard now loaded with a page and a half of disaster, took the floor. "If we're agreed, I will circulate the assignments for the night's patrols and open channels for real-time reporting. No improvisation. No heroics. If you're down a team member, you report it. We cannot afford any more unaccounted assets."

She let the words settle, then moved to the next item. Vincent watched the room as the tension eased: Germans whispered, Frenchmen plotted, Modernisers huddled around a laptop, Traditionalists bristled at the thought of change.

Vincent tried to focus on the present, but his mind kept drifting to Ren, to Zara's spectral lectures, to the way Mrs Barley's pen never stopped. He thought about the way every meeting, every moment of hope, always seemed to end with a list of the dead.

He thought about his own name, and whether it would outlast the next night.

He took a sip of the boiling mug, wincing at the burn. It was almost enough to distract him from the creeping certainty that this was the last time he'd see so many of the faces in this room.

He looked at Ren, who finally looked back. She tried a smile, and it almost worked.

Vincent raised his mug in a silent toast, and for the briefest second, the war room felt like a family, or something adjacent to one.

The moment passed. Assignments were distributed, and the room emptied in orderly bursts, leaving only the ghosts and the quiet, blue flames.

Vincent lingered, staring into the dark, waiting for the next battle to write itself.

# EIGHTEEN

It was a quarter past nothing, in the haunted hour between late-night kebab and early-morning shame, when Vincent, Mrs Barley, and Ren huddled in the flat and watched Zara slowly fail to exist.

The room, never a spacious environment even by South London standards, had become a funhouse of shadows. The only light came from a trio of guttering candles, one of which had long since declared bankruptcy and collapsed into its own wax. Their combined effort managed to cast more smoke than illumination, so every surface in the place—from battered table to overcrowded bookshelf—seemed to wriggle in and out of definition. This was not helped by the literal layers of prophecy scrolls, scrapbooks, and defunct magical implements that carpeted the floor.

Zara's ghost flickered at the head of the table, her outline alternately solid as old enamel and then, a moment later, gone thin and blurry as an afterimage.

Her hands were less hands than probability. Sometimes they hovered over a text, fingers splayed as if prepping to flick it off the edge of reality; sometimes they drifted above the page like a hand forgotten in a lift. When she leaned in, the air went thirty degrees colder and the candles guttered, as if the universe wanted to look away but couldn't decide on an exit.

Ren perched on a kitchen stool, hands jammed under her thighs so they wouldn't do anything embarrassing like start shaking. Mrs Barley occupied the only upright chair, her back an unyielding wall of administrative fortitude. Vincent paced. He'd tried to do it in a casual way, but the room was too small and the tension too thick: every five steps, he'd rebound off the bookshelf, sending an avalanche of prophecy scrap down the spine and onto the carpet.

"Stop that," Zara said, her voice not quite in sync with the movement of her mouth. "You're making the ectoplasm in here look undignified."

Vincent stopped, but not because of the reprimand. "You're glitching," he said, and gestured at the part of Zara's face that kept doubling and undoubling, like a VHS tape gone sticky. "That new, or just for our benefit?"

Zara blinked, then checked her reflection in the shiny curve of the kettle. She frowned. "Could be worse. I had a client once who kept waking up in the wrong body. At least my failures are consistent." She turned to Mrs Barley, who scribbled this down with the efficiency of a prison doctor at inoculation time. "You ready for the actual briefing, or do you want to keep watching me dissolve?"

Mrs Barley didn't look up. "We're all ears, Miss Delacourt."

"Good. Because time is not on our side." Zara gestured at

the detritus on the table, and the prophecies rearranged them-selves in a fast, sullen shuffle. "You're here about the Draft. The thing eating the city. The thing that nearly rewrote Ren out of existence and made Parliament look like the world's worst Bring Your Daughter to Work Day."

Ren made a noise that, in a different universe, might have been a laugh. "At least it's on brand," she muttered.

Zara pointed at Ren's scar. "Ren might be safe now, but the connection is still active. If Ashcroft succeeds, or if the coalition fails to hold the perimeter, the Draft will go full viral. Not just a vampire story. Not just London. Everything. Because the Draft doesn't want to control the world—it wants to *be* the world."

She let this land, the silence padded only by the faint crackle of burning wick and Vincent's jaw grinding out a Morse code of impatience.

Mrs Barley said, "You're suggesting the entity's root is not localised."

"I'm suggesting," said Zara, "that the root is nowhere. And everywhere. If you want to kill it, you have to go outside the plot."

Ren blinked. "You mean, like... leave the city?"

Zara shook her head. The afterimage trailed a beat behind, catching up only when she stopped. "Not the city, darling. The narrative."

Vincent, who'd gone back to pacing, laughed without humour. "Brilliant. I can barely handle going to IKEA on a Saturday, and now you want us to spelunk my subconscious."

Zara grinned, or what passed for it on a ghost. "Not yours, specifically. But yes, you're headed for the hollow. The Draft's nest is in the negative space between stories. A cave in the wall of reality, built from centuries of hunger, rage, and memory. It's ugly in there. Most things don't come back."

Ren bit her lip, and for a moment the tremor in her hands threatened to make it above the table. "So, we're all volunteers for the deep dive. Who's bringing the picnic?"

Mrs Barley cleared her throat with the dry authority of a bailiff. "What are the operational requirements?"

Zara looked at her clipboard, then at Mrs Barley. "First, you'll need an anchor. Someone, or something, to keep your bodies tethered. Second, you'll need a bridge—preferably a vampire with enough existential baggage to punch through the wall. Third, you'll need to bring something the Draft can't predict. A wildcard." She turned to Ren. "You, obviously."

Ren snorted. "Because I'm unkillable?"

"Because you're unpredictable," Zara said. "Everything else down there is on repeat."

Vincent stopped pacing. "And what about you?"

Zara shrugged, or tried to. Her shoulder flickered, then reconstituted itself a few inches out of alignment. "I'll get you in. But I can't promise I'll make it back out."

"You said that when we went into Carmine's library." Vincent said.

"This time it's not for dramatic effect."

The words hung in the air, heavy as wet cement.

Mrs Barley made a note. "What's the exit protocol?"

"Don't die," said Zara. "Or if you do, try to make it memorable. The Draft hates surprises."

The candles, as if on cue, guttered lower. Shadows surged in from the corners, thickening the air. Vincent paced again, faster, fingers twitching at the edge of his sleeves. The canines he usually kept so neatly capped now glinted in the candlelight, a low-grade threat or maybe just a side effect of stress.

"Let's say we make it to the centre," he said. "What's there? Ashcroft, or something worse?"

Zara's mouth twitched. "Ashcroft's the host. The Draft's the parasite. But at the core, you'll find the source. The original story. If you can rewrite it—burn it, break it, edit it out—you might take the whole system down."

Ren looked at Vincent, then at Mrs Barley, who was still writing with a face of perfect calm.

Vincent met her gaze. "You in?"

Ren bared her fangs—a new trick, but already well-practised. "If you don't chicken out first."

He grinned, but the grin didn't last.

Mrs Barley put down her pen. "We go at sundown. I'll organise the anchor team. Miss Delacourt, you'll need to prepare the bridge."

Zara saluted, the gesture glitching at the elbow. "Already on it, chief."

The meeting adjourned in the same tempo as a firing squad: fast, final, and no time for goodbyes. Ren hung back, watching the others file toward the door.

Vincent paused at the threshold. "You sure you're up for it?" he said, voice so soft it barely carried.

Zara smiled, a real one this time, and her eyes went old and tired and a little proud. "I'm dead already, Vincent. I'll be fine."

He nodded, then left.

Ren lingered. She looked at Zara, at the room, at the mess of papers and the dying candlelight.

"You really think we can do it?" she asked.

Zara considered. "No. But that's never stopped you before."

Ren smiled, and left.

When the flat emptied, Zara let her outline blur, let her fingers fade in and out of the parchment. She waited until the candles were down to stumps, then drifted to the window, watched the city seethe and glitter in the predawn.

She made a silent wish for her idiot friends, then turned back to her books.

It was going to be a long day.

They staged the apocalypse in a warehouse next to the Camberwell Sainsbury's. The coalition—never officially named, but unofficially called The Doomed by anyone with an eye for branding—had colonised the shell of the old Bevan & Sons furniture depot, a building whose primary assets were square footage and plausible deniability. From the outside, it looked like a place you'd go to buy an off-brand mattress or, failing that, to die quietly of exposure. Inside, the air hummed with the static of a hundred clashing preparations: the ceremonial, the martial, and the sort of high-stakes DIY that had kept Britain running since 1942.

The Modernisers had set up a command post in what had once been the office manager's fishbowl, now repurposed as a tech altar to the Algorithmic Age. Studio lights hung from the ceiling in a sort of digital mistletoe, illuminating Aurelia Voss as she marshalled her followers with crisp hand signals and the clinical detachment of a surgeon prepping for field amputation.

Cass drifted between the screens, his thumbs a blur as he beta-tested blood-detection apps and crowdsourced tips on vampiric countermeasures from several dozen online "consultants." The windowsill bristled with enchanted drones—each one blinking a different shade of Instagram-ready cyan—while a series of tablets, laptops, and repurposed smart home devices watched everything in slow, deliberate horror.

The Traditionalists had taken over the far end of the warehouse, fencing themselves off with actual velvet rope and a line of gold-plated stanchions that nobody admitted to owning. Their elders sat in stately rows, oiling and sharpening ancestral silverware in the flickering glow of real candles. Each knife and fork underwent a series of rites: wiped, balanced, aligned to the nearest half-millimetre, then laid to rest on starched white linen. This was not for show. Every item would go into battle, whether as impromptu weapon, magical focus, or evidence at a future inquiry. When they prayed, it was to the God of Precedent, and every Amen sounded like a line item in an unbreakable will.

The German contingent—thin on numbers, heavy on discipline—had converted a section of the loading dock into a war room. Falkenhayn's lieutenants inspected weapons, bandaged wounds, and drilled their squads with the grim efficiency of men who'd stopped believing in miracles before puberty. The French detachment, predictably, had set up a mini-bistro next to the fire exit, complete with a selection of forbidden cheeses and at least three varieties of absinthe. Marquis Deveraux and his lieutenants wore the ceremonial sashes of the Parisian Vampire Court, though the effect was somewhat diluted by the fact that most of them were already sloshed. They alternated between toasting the coming slaughter and muttering darkly about betrayal and ennui.

In the dead centre of the warehouse, under a single halogen bulb that flickered with the timing of a dying star, stood Ren. She'd spent the last hour in a makeshift training circle—a ring of old traffic cones and caution tape—testing the limits of her new, unwanted hardware. At first she'd kept it simple: push-ups, sprints, the sort of thing you did to convince yourself the old body was still in there, somewhere under the monster. It hadn't taken long to outpace the living, then the undead, then the plausible. Now she was standing in front of a battered folding chair, gripping the frame with both hands, willing herself to *not* snap it in half.

The chair lost.

It crumpled, sending splinters and flakes of blue paint across the caution tape. For a second, Ren stared at the wreckage, half-tempted to try again, then laughed. It was a thin, nervous sound, but it didn't break. She brushed the debris from her jeans and glanced up at the balcony, where Vincent leaned on the railing like the last judge of X Factor.

He gave her a slow, ironic clap. "That's my girl," he called, voice echoing off the metal rafters.

She grinned. "You want a turn, old man?"

Vincent shrugged, then shimmied down the staircase with a predatory grace that would've been less unsettling if he didn't have four centuries of homicide in his CV. He landed a few feet away from Ren and appraised the remains of the chair.

"I always preferred something with a bit more structural integrity," he said, then pointed at a concrete pylon. "Try that."

Ren eyed the column. "You just want to see if I break my arm."

He bared his fangs in a not-quite-smile. "Only one way to find out."

From the upper level, Mrs Barley watched with a look of polite indifference that did nothing to hide the fact she was mentally drafting next-of-kin notifications. She ticked off a line on her clipboard, then descended the steps, flanked by two Trad elders carrying a crate of what looked suspiciously like ceremonial shot glasses.

Mrs Barley's stride cut through the room like a guillotine at a birthday party. She stopped in front of Vincent and Ren, eyed the wrecked chair, and said, "If you're finished playing, there's a briefing in five. The Germans have agreed to not invade the French section until the meeting is over."

Vincent saluted. "Wouldn't want to start another world war."

Cass appeared, trailing a cloud of Modernisers and the faint tang of synthetic lavender. "Can we do a dry run of the communication protocols first?" he asked, aiming a phone at Mrs Barley's head. "The signal in here is absolute arse."

Mrs Barley did not sigh, but only by force of will. "Use the staff Wi-Fi. Password is 'inevitability.' Please don't change it again, or I will staple your tongue to the ethernet cable."

Cass beamed. "On it, chief." He sauntered off, typing as he went, and nearly collided with a German orderly carrying a box of grenade-shaped amulets.

Ren rolled her eyes. "Is it always like this?" she asked Vincent.

He watched Cass go. "Pretty much. Until it gets worse."

The next five minutes belonged to Mrs Barley, who corralled the coalition into a semi-orderly assembly on the main floor. She took the dais, ignored the feedback from the ancient speaker system, and addressed the crowd with the authority of a woman who had survived three pandemics and four administrative reorganisations.

"The enemy," she said, "remains Ashcroft and his patchwork army. The objective: disrupt the Draft's narrative at the root, or at least buy enough time for Zara's team to breach the core. We are outnumbered, outgunned, and out-funded, but we have one thing Ashcroft will never have."

She paused. "A functional Operations department."

This drew actual laughter from the Germans, polite clapping from the French, and a round of ironic applause from the Modernisers.

Mrs Barley continued, "You have your assignments. Teams one and two hit the front. Three and four will flank. Modernisers, you're on drone surveillance and comms. Any unauthorised rewrites or breaches of reality should be flagged and, if possible, filmed for future training purposes." She let the last part hang, a thread of sarcasm strong enough to anchor the entire plan.

She eyed Ren. "Team Five, you're with Mr Lupo and myself. Zara will brief you on your insertion once we arrive."

Ren saluted with the wrong hand, realised, then switched. Mrs Barley barely blinked.

The crowd dispersed. Vincent lingered with Ren, who tried not to look too nervous but couldn't quite stop glancing at the loading bay doors.

"Relax," Vincent said. "It's just another night in hell."

Ren ran a hand through her hair, then looked at him sideways. "You scared?"

He didn't answer right away. Then, "I'm terrified. But not of Ashcroft."

She smiled. "Good. Means you're not dead inside yet."

He smirked, then nodded at the stairs. "Let's get the last rites from Zara. Before the Germans eat all the good bread."

They found Zara's ghost near the fire exit, giving last-minute instructions to a ring of Modernisers and Mrs Barley's senior admin. She was more solid than she'd been in days, her edges crisp, her expression running somewhere between proud aunt and gunner in the trenches. When she saw Ren and Vincent, she dismissed the others with a flick of her hand.

Zara fixed Ren with a stare that cut through the bravado. "You understand what happens if this goes wrong?"

Ren nodded. "I stop existing. Or worse, I get rebooted as a cameo in Ashcroft's fanfic."

Zara almost smiled. "Exactly. So don't fuck it up."

Vincent crossed his arms. "And if *I* fuck it up?"

Zara's voice went cool. "Then you do what you always do. Improvise, and pray you don't take the rest of us with you."

Mrs Barley arrived, checked her watch, and raised an eyebrow at the trio. "Time."

Zara's form flickered, just for a second. "All right," she said. "You know your way in. Once you cross the breach, there's no coming back except through."

Vincent looked at Ren. "Ready?"

Ren drew a breath, then let it go slow. "Not in this life."

He grinned. "Then let's see what's next."

The group moved out, single file, into the night.

In the warehouse, the teams fell in behind them. Falkenhayn and Deveraux paused at the threshold, shared a look, then clinked glasses in a silent, lethal toast. Aurelia and Cass gathered their ring-lit flock, while the Trad elders moved with the solemn efficiency of pallbearers who'd already chosen their own grave.

At the exit, Mrs Barley handed Vincent a stack of paperwork—last will, power of attorney, one-page "absentee" protocol. "If you die, I'll mark you absent," she said, voice utterly bland. "Don't make me do extra paperwork."

Vincent barked a laugh, pocketed the forms, and led the charge into the dark.

Behind them, the warehouse hummed with the restless energy of a city about to flip the switch between order and oblivion.

Ahead, the night waited, teeth bared, stories ready.

The end, as always, would write itself.

# NINETEEN

Midnight in London was not so much a time as an ecological niche, and the abandoned churchyard behind St Mary's provided the optimal environment for rare and endangered rituals. The team gathered in the weed-clogged cloisters, the perimeter of the old graveyard hemmed in by iron railings and the sort of CCTV cameras that mostly served to document how quickly the neighbours could forget the dead.

It was cold, but not the ordinary urban chill—a supernatural draught bled through the stones, so every breath arrived as a white-out exhale, lingering in the air like regrets. The gravestones here had long since given up the fight with entropy, their names and dates reduced to shallow scars, their top halves eroded by centuries of atmospheric indifference. A few were still legible if you squinted, but most just slumped against one another, shoulder to shoulder like casualties of a pub brawl who'd forgotten what they were fighting about.

The Modernisers had sent an advance party to dress the

place, so the central crypt was ringed with what looked like a commemorative candle display but was, in fact, a ritual circle meticulously plotted to within two centimetres on a spreadsheet. There were no white pillar candles here—only black, poured from a paraffin blend so dense it absorbed even the meagre moonlight. The wicks were pre-soaked in blessed gin and each sat in a custom-etched holder. The flames, once lit, didn't so much burn as hover, blue-white and unblinking, immune to the wind. A few looked like they were floating independently of their wax base.

Vincent, Mrs Barley, and Ren entered as a unit, each carrying the residue of the week's earlier disasters: mud on their boots, blood on their sleeves, and the kind of haunted eye that made even the pigeons cross the path to avoid them. Vincent had dressed for the occasion—dark suit, collar open, tie abandoned somewhere on the way—but his attempt at composure was ruined by the bandage peeking from beneath his cuff and the way he kept rubbing his jaw, as if hoping to dislodge the memory of what he'd had to do.

Ren looked worse, but in a way that suggested she was proud of it. The hoodie was shredded from the shoulder to the wrist, exposing the scar on her forearm like a fresh tattoo, and her eyes, already shifted a few shades towards inhuman, caught every glint from the candles and magnified it. She moved with the loose, predatory grace of someone still learning how to walk without putting her fist through the scenery. Every time a crow cawed from a rooftop, she flinched and bared her teeth in reflex.

Mrs Barley, umbrella tucked under one arm, radiated such absolute confidence that the dead leaves on the path seemed to re-arrange themselves to avoid contact with her shoes. She had brought a backup clipboard and was already annotating the events as they happened, her pen ticking at double time. The Moderniser and Traditionalist factions had sent a combined honour guard—Aurelia and Cass at the front, Deveraux and Falkenhayn's seconds close behind. Even the German and French contingents, still licking their wounds from the previous evening's massacre, fell silent as the three arrived.

At the dead centre of the circle, Zara's ghost floated. All week, she'd been fading in and out with the whimsy of a dodgy Wi-Fi signal; now she hovered, locked in place, a pale corona of her former self. The colour had all gone from her hair, the lines of her face more carved than drawn, and her body was a suggestion rather than a shape. She glowed the colour of freezer burn, more absent than present, and the air for a metre in all directions shimmered like cheap Perspex.

She did not look at Vincent or Mrs Barley or Ren. Instead, her attention was fixed on the gravestones, her hands moving in loops and spirals, conducting the candlelight as if it were a very slow and easily offended orchestra.

"Everyone inside the ring," she said. Her voice was the only thing that hadn't faded; it echoed across the crypt with the authority of a headmistress breaking up a sixth form riot. "We're starting."

No one hesitated. The survivors found places along the circumference, Modernisers north, Traditionalists south, French and Germans on either flank, and the English in the gaps, as always. Ren, Vincent, and Mrs Barley took their place beside Zara, whose outline flickered as they crossed the perimeter. The air inside the circle was somehow even colder. Vincent felt the hair on his arms stand up, followed by the more concerning sensation of the skin itself trying to migrate off his bones.

Zara wasted no time. "Don't speak," she said, eyes still on the stones. "Don't look back. Everything here wants to be remembered."

She began to recite: not a single language, but three or four at once, the phrases spilling over each other, sometimes Latin, sometimes a noise that sounded like a dial-up modem choking on a curse. The candles responded: first flickering, then stretching, the flames bending sideways to lick at the old names carved into the grave markers. As she spoke, the inscriptions began to move, the letters detaching from their lines and crawling across the limestone like a parade of glow-worms. Vincent tried not to watch, but the way the dates re-ordered themselves—years jumping forward and back, first names swapping with last— made it hard to look away.

Ren didn't even try. Her eyes tracked every crawling letter, every shift in the shadows. If the scar on her arm bothered her, she gave no sign, but her jaw was clenched so hard the veins on her neck stood out like blue-black wires. Vincent saw her right hand flex, then dig into her palm, drawing blood. He'd have said something, but Zara's warning echoed in his mind: *Don't speak. Don't look back.*

Mrs Barley kept her head forward, but her pen continued its frantic note-taking. If she noticed the way the candles had formed a pentagram at her feet, or that the nearest stone now bore her own name (with a best-before date ten years hence), she gave no outward sign.

The ritual went on for a minute or an hour; time inside the circle was as meaningless as the names on the stones. At some point, Vincent lost track of the other teams. He tried to count the candles, but the number never stayed the same. Every so often, he caught a glimpse of Cass's ring light through the fog, or heard Aurelia's laugh—high, clear, echoing—but it all came muffled, as if underwater.

The crawling inscriptions reached their zenith. Now the words weren't just moving; they were rewriting. In place of faded epitaphs, the stones spelled out messages, sometimes in English, sometimes in that twitchy, modem-language Zara had used. Some were warnings: ABANDON HOPE, MEMORY IS A WEAPON, DO NOT LET IT WRITE YOU. Others seemed like private jokes, or errors in translation: BAD SEED, WRONG DRAFT, THE BUREAUCRACY WILL DEVOUR ALL.

Vincent's own stone now read: VINCENT LUPO, 1330–∞. FAMOUSLY POOR DECISIONS.

He wanted to laugh, but the air had grown too thick for it. The wind, so biting before, stilled to absolute nothing. Even the city noises—the taxis, the sirens, the students staggering home from clubs—faded to a dead hush.

And then Zara stopped speaking. She looked up, eyes locking first with Ren, then Vincent, then Mrs Barley.

"Ready?" she asked.

Ren nodded, not trusting her voice. Vincent followed suit, though he felt anything but.

Mrs Barley said, "Proceed," and it was the least nervous thing anyone had ever said in a haunted churchyard.

Zara stretched out her hands, fingers fragmenting at the tips, and made a tearing gesture in the air. The world in front of them split, a vertical seam opening from the ground up, wider and wider until it became a rip in the fabric of everything. There was no sound, just a snap in the back of the mind, and then the space between the seams was black—absolute, featureless black, so deep that even the candlelight seemed afraid to trespass.

The gap yawned, and the only thing Vincent could think of was that it looked like a book with every page torn out, a hollow spine and nothing else.

The Germans, French, Traditionalists and Modernisers led the way. Ren went next, hunger written all over her but chin up, eyes forward. She stepped to the edge of the tear, looked back at no one, and vanished in a shimmer.

Vincent was next. He hesitated, just a second, then followed, hands fisted so tight the bones popped. The chill on the other side pulled him in.

Mrs Barley waited a full beat, then marched through, umbrella out like a sabre.

Zara's ghost watched them go, her own outline flickering out just before the seam sealed shut.

The churchyard was empty.

The world beyond, not so much.

The first step in the void was a mistake, but it was the only one on offer. Vincent landed with a jolt and was rewarded by the sensation of his insides being wrung through a mangle. For a beat, there was nothing—no sense of up, down, or even the expectation of gravity—but then the world spun out and slammed into place, and he realised he was standing at the edge of something vast and ancient and wrong.

He was in a cathedral, or the memory of one, stretched to impossible scale and built from materials that had never existed outside of nightmares or the more ambitious urban renewal projects. The ceiling, if it existed, was out of reach—just a press of darkness occasionally shot through with flickers of movement, like distant trains behind smoked glass. The walls curved upwards, covered in the arterial red of pulsing veins, each line throbbing with a heartbeat that was not his own. The light was everywhere and nowhere: sometimes brilliant, sometimes black as the inside of a shut coffin, always shifting, as if reality had contracted an aggressive strain of vertigo and was refusing all medication.

The floor was not a floor but a living thing, soft and rubbery, undulating in slow, queasy swells. Every footstep threatened to pitch Vincent off-balance, and it took all his will to plant himself, to remember that up and down still meant something even here. The air was thick, syrupy, the taste of iron and burning paper, and every time he tried to breathe his lungs threatened to cough up something vital.

The only constant was the sound: a whispering, at first soft, then growing into a cacophony of overlapping voices. Not echo, not memory, but something worse: the distinct sensation of being surrounded by versions of himself, each one muttering a different script, a different set of failures and betrayals. They overlapped and tangled, a crowd of Vincents, all competing to see who could be most disappointing.

He heard himself as tyrant—voice deep, dripping with the satisfaction of meeting out punishment. He heard himself as coward, weeping apologies into the dirt, scrabbling for the nearest exit. He heard himself as monster, gorged on blood and glory, roaring at the void until it roared back and devoured him whole.

He stumbled forward, one hand out, the other clenched to keep from punching himself in the head. Ren appeared at his left, eyes wide and alert, nostrils flared as if scenting the architecture. Her new senses—whatever they were—seemed to thrive here. She didn't walk so much as stalk, every motion controlled, precise, a predator among wounded prey. The hunger was on her, a low growl vibrating under the skin, but she held it together.

Mrs Barley took the rear, umbrella at her side, walking with the same authority she'd used to corral bureaucrats and monsters alike. She didn't blink, didn't waver, but Vincent caught her glancing upwards, as if checking for snipers or other, less human threats.

Ren stopped him with a hand on his shoulder. The contact was electric—a bolt of pure need—and he almost lashed out before remembering who he was, and who she was, and what it meant that they were both still here.

"You good?" she asked, her voice cutting through the Vincent-chorus.

He tried to reply, but all that came out was, "Which one?"

Ren's grip tightened, fingers digging in with supernatural strength. "The one that doesn't quit."

He almost laughed, but the echoes around them gobbled the sound and spat it back as a thousand derisive snorts.

"Keep moving," said Mrs Barley, her own voice slicing through the fog. "It gets worse if you stop."

They pressed on, the ground slithering beneath them, the walls breathing in and out with impossible lungs. Occasionally, Vincent saw flashes in the dark: scenes from his life, twisted and stretched, always ending in disaster. Here was himself on the ramparts at Smolensk, howling for blood and getting it, but then losing the plot and the city and half his people in the bargain. There he was in Florence, trying to play the diplomat, only to end up a side character in someone else's coup. Every failure, every collapse, paraded before him in high definition and surround sound.

The others weren't spared. Vincent glimpsed Ren, her face contorted in a feral snarl, standing over a pile of bodies, jaws slicked in arterial red. He saw Mrs Barley, stone-faced and perfect, calmly signing her name to a ledger as a line of civilians were marched to their deaths, her pen dipped in what he was sure was fresh blood. The visions came and went, so fast and so dense he started to wonder if he'd ever left the real world, or if this was just what passed for a Monday morning in his head.

They reached a rise in the floor, a lump of congealed darkness that might have once been a pulpit or a speaker's dais. The whispers got louder, overlapping so intensely that for a moment Vincent felt his own thoughts dissolving, leaking out of his ears. He fell to one knee, grinding his teeth, and saw the Mark on Ren's arm flaring like a beacon, casting a strobe of blue-white onto the living walls.

The voices congealed into a single, overwhelming presence.

*"You cannot win,"* said the voice. It was Vincent's, but also not: deeper, heavier, as if layered with every regret he'd ever refused to own. *"You are only what you are written to be."*

Ren stood over him, her own face flickering through a series of expressions—fear, rage, hunger, then a cold, diamond-hard resolve.

She knelt, grabbed Vincent by the collar, and hauled him upright. "It's not real," she said, and for a second it was Ren's old voice—the one from before, the one that could shut down a lecture hall or clear a pub. "It's a draft. It only wins if you let it."

He looked at her, at the Mark, at the way her skin was almost translucent in this anti-light, and wondered if she'd really survived, or if he'd brought her to hell just to watch her rot from the inside.

He found his footing, and together they turned to face the voice.

At the far end of the cathedral, a shape was forming: huge, formless, built from layered scraps of paper and unfinished sentences. It writhed, shifting from one outline to another—sometimes a man in a judge's wig, sometimes a woman with a scythe, sometimes just a gnashing maw lined with endless rows of shark-like teeth. The surface of the thing crawled with faces, all of them familiar, all of them Vincent's at some age or another, all of them screaming.

Mrs Barley strode ahead, umbrella out, chin high.

"What's the play?" asked Vincent, still half-crouched.

"Don't let it write the ending," she said, as if that answered everything.

The entity—the Draft Eternal, Vincent supposed—rumbled, the sound vibrating up through his bones. Its teeth clacked in anticipation, the pages of its body fluttering like a library in a hurricane.

It spoke again, this time in a voice so huge it rattled the

cathedral's walls: *You are footnotes. You are errors. You will be corrected.*

Ren bared her fangs, a gesture so automatic and so new it almost made Vincent proud. "Fuck that," she said, and for a moment, the voices in his head flinched.

Vincent stood straight. The old pain was there, but so was something else—a memory of every time he'd survived, every time he'd got up when he should have stayed down. He squared his shoulders and addressed the Draft.

"Footnotes are what keep the story honest," he said, voice steady. "And every editor hates a plot hole."

The Draft reeled, its shape collapsing in on itself, then re-forming as something even bigger, even less coherent. Now it was part ink-stained serpent, part parliamentary bench, part open grave. The air filled with the stink of ozone and fresh blood, and the ground rippled as if it was about to throw them off like so many fleas.

Ren locked eyes with Vincent, and he saw in her a terrifying confidence. "We end it," she said. "Here."

Mrs Barley nodded, her own Mark flaring as she raised the umbrella and pointed it directly at the heart of the monster.

The Draft, perhaps sensing the breach, surged forward, mouth open to reveal a spinning maw of shredded paper and grinding bone. The voices doubled, tripled, each one pleading, bargaining, screaming for recognition.

Vincent lunged, grabbed Ren's hand, and together they charged the dais. The closer they got, the more the air pressed back—each step a battle against gravity, against their own will to fold and surrender. The scar on Ren's arm bled white light, burning the living floor, and the effect was immediate: wherever the light struck, the fabric of the void hissed, recoiled, split.

Mrs Barley joined them, matching their pace, her umbrella now sparking with angry blue energy. Vincent felt the world contract, then expand, then twist as the Draft tried to re-write them out of existence with every step.

It didn't work.

Ren was first to the pulpit. She drove her fist into the thing's face—her own face, briefly, before the illusion collapsed. Vincent followed, driving his own punch into the mass, feeling bone and paper and something softer give way. Mrs Barley jabbed the umbrella into the core, twisting hard.

The Draft howled, every unfinished story it had ever devoured screaming through the hall. The visions around them went berserk—hundreds of possible Vincents, Ren's, Mrs Barleys, all living and dying and being erased in fast-forward, none of them lasting more than a heartbeat.

The entity bucked, then started to collapse, the pages shrivelling to ash, the teeth snapping and then shattering. The ground beneath them steadied; the air cleared. For a second, it seemed they might be able to breathe again.

But the monster wasn't done. Even as it shrank, it pulled them in, dragging them towards the centre, towards a point of absolute density—a singularity of every error, every missed chance, every line that had never made it to print.

Vincent looked at Ren, at Mrs Barley, and knew what was coming. They had to finish it.

He stepped into the breach, letting the gravity take him, and at the last moment, he seized the central page—the original story, the root of it all.

It was blank.

He stared at the empty space, at the line waiting to be filled. He heard the voices clamour for an answer, for a name, for an ending.

Vincent grinned, let the old arrogance bloom, and scrawled across the page with his own blood:

NOT THE END.

The void howled, and the world snapped shut.

# TWENTY

Vincent stumbled into the next circle of hell, which announced itself with a stench of fresh blood and a humidity usually reserved for slaughterhouses on a bank holiday. The walls closed in, closer now, their surfaces throbbing in synchrony with his pulse, every vein on the stone a luminous artery. A droplet of red condensed on the low-hanging ceiling, then splattered onto his shoulder, where it sizzled through the fabric and sent a convulsion down his spine. He wiped it away, only to find the patch on his skin healed immediately, leaving nothing but the aftertaste of metal and humiliation.

The floor was worse. It undulated, viscous and soft, as though the entire chamber were the inside of a living heart. Each step squelched. Each step resisted, as if the cavern wanted to pin him in place and digest him at its leisure.

He pressed on, because forward was the only direction that didn't involve being eaten alive by his own footprints.

The space opened into a cavernous amphitheatre, but the

seats were occupied only by empty suits of armour, each one bearing his own face, each one twisted into a rictus of agony or ecstasy or both. They watched him with a predator's blankness. He tried not to look, but the eyes tracked him, followed his shamble toward the stage, where three figures already waited.

Not revenants. Not the reanimated bureaucrats he'd come to expect from the Draft's theatre of cruelty.

No. The three on the stage were Vincent. Different models, different tragedies, all manufactured to specification.

The first: a wolf, or what the London press might have called a wolf if they'd ever seen one outside of a fairy tale. Its fur was streaked with gore, matted and patchy, claws yellow and cracked, muzzle crusted with black and red. It circled, hackles raised, eyes rimmed with a sickly gold that pulsed in time with the room. When it bared its teeth, the fangs were human, and when it opened its mouth, it howled in a voice that was unmistakably his own.

The second: a man on a throne, or what passed for a throne here—three dozen femurs lashed together with barbed wire, cushions made from the shorn scalps of the just and the unjust alike. This Vincent wore a velvet smoking jacket, but the silk was charred and stained; he reclined with one leg over the arm, a glass of blood in his hand and a smirk that reeked of someone who'd never missed a chance to gloat. His face was cleaner, but the eyes were dead, long since replaced by the cold coinage of power.

The third: a wraith, thin to the point of transparency, hunched in on itself, arms wrapped around its knees. It looked up only to flinch, then looked away, muttering to itself about the futility of movement and the inevitability of being devoured.

Vincent eyed the tableau and fought the urge to roll his own eyes out of his head and onto the floor, just to avoid watching.

The wolf pounced first, landing directly in front of him, jaws stretched wide. "You could have been a king," it said, spittle flecking his face. "You could have feasted for eternity, but you squandered it on cowardice and self-pity. How does it feel, Vincent, to know the animal is all that's left?"

He wiped the mess from his cheek. "At least I don't lick my own arse in public."

The wolf's snarl doubled, and it slashed at him with a paw the size of a Sunday roast, but the blow passed through Vincent like a strong wind—cold, but insubstantial. He barely registered the impact.

The second Vincent—call him the Monarch—leaned in, glass poised at the lip. "Always the rebel, never the ruler. Do you know how many times you were offered the world, old friend? Do you know how many turned it down?" He raised the glass, then drank, the liquid swirling inside with the slow gravity of despair. "Every story ends the same. You sabotage it. You kill it before it can kill you."

The third Vincent—call him the Ghost—never lifted his head, just rocked back and forth, whispering, "They're all watching. They'll never forgive you. They'll never let you go. Even if you leave, you'll never be anywhere but here."

Vincent felt the words land, heavier than the claws or the ridicule. The room was silent, except for the chorus of his own voices, overlapping with the Draft's omnipresent hiss.

"Every story ends with you a monster," they said, and this time it was not one, but all three in perfect unison. The empty suits in the amphitheatre picked up the line and repeated it, their jaws clacking as they sang the refrain.

He laughed, or tried to, but the sound bounced back at him warped, as though every echo was being processed through a meat grinder. He reached into his pocket for a cigarette, found nothing, then shrugged and let the next line come.

"If you're my existential crisis, you're running low on budget," he said. "I've seen better special effects on late-night telly."

The wolf lunged again, and this time, Vincent lashed out—fingers bent into claws, the better to answer in kind. He raked at the beast's snout, but his hands passed through, scraping only the illusion. He kept slashing, desperate to feel anything solid, but it was like fighting his own reflection in a filthy mirror.

The Monarch rose from the throne, the bones creaking. "You can't kill what you already are, Vincent. You are the Draft's favourite error. The footnote that becomes the headline. You think you can escape, but you keep coming back here, don't you?"

The Ghost whimpered, hands over its head. "It never ends. It never ends. It never—"

Vincent spun, planted his heel in the dirt, and swung at the Monarch with a right hook that should have shattered a jaw. Instead, his fist exploded into shards of memory: faces of every vampire, every human, every idiot he'd ever failed to save. The pieces fluttered away like a bad confetti, and where the Monarch stood was only smoke, coiling into the shape of a crown.

The wolf circled, now behind him, jaws at his neck. "You're

not even a monster. You're just a story about a monster. What a waste."

He bared his own fangs and turned, sinking his teeth into the shadow-wolf's throat. The taste was brackish and cold, the texture somewhere between ink and silk. It bucked, then dissolved, reappearing a yard away, unharmed, licking imaginary wounds and laughing.

From the walls, the Draft Eternal sang a higher harmony: *You will be corrected. You will be rewritten.*

He screamed at the voice, but the sound splintered. The Ghost clung to his legs, dragging him down to the pulsing floor, where the heartbeat pressed up through his back and into his brain.

The Monarch returned, one hand on Vincent's head, forcing him to kneel. "This is the best part," it said. "The collapse. The punchline. The last page, and the monster always loses."

Vincent twisted, tried to break the grip, but the Monarch's hand was welded to his scalp, nails digging through the skin to the bone beneath. The wolf pinned his right arm, the Ghost his left, and all three bore down, mouths open, ready to devour the last of him.

He howled, not in fear, but in pure, animal frustration. He kicked, bucked, spat every curse he could remember. The echo-selves laughed, the Monarch louder than the rest. "Look at you. All teeth, no bite. All bravado, no backbone. In the end, you're just like us."

Vincent stopped fighting.

He hung limp, letting the weight of his own shadows bear

him down. The heartbeat in the floor grew stronger, the Draft's presence threading into every synapse.

*You are footnotes. You are errors.*

He shuddered, every nerve afire with the pain of memory, of knowing he was nothing but a flawed copy of a flawed original. The three echoes closed in, their faces merging, their hands clawing at his skin. They leaned in, teeth to throat, ready to finish the job.

He closed his eyes, braced for erasure.

And then—

And then, from somewhere outside the circle, a voice. Sharp, unbroken, a single syllable that cut through the misery like a razor:

"No."

The echoes paused, jaws hovering just above his neck. The cavern light shifted, the heartbeat staggered. The amphitheatre suits rattled as they all turned, seeking out the source.

The voice came again, stronger. "Not this time."

And for a moment, Vincent recognised it. Not his own. Not the Draft's.

Ren's.

Ren's new eyes drank the dark, and she wasn't afraid. She stood on the pulpit-dais of the cathedral-void, ankles deep in a membrane of something that wanted to be water but stank of ink, and old wounds. The space thrummed with subsonic threat, a pressure in the jaw, and a chorus of Vincent's voices echoing off the living stone: versions of him in all possible genres, some tragic, some farce, some the sort of draft no one would ever show an editor.

But the trick of the place, she realised, was that it worked on everyone. Her own reflection stalked her now—a version from a life she'd never lived, the one where she'd accepted the Mark's voice and let it narrate her into oblivion. This Ren wore a Parliament-issue suit, too big for her, too old; the skin beneath was webbed in black, the veins thick as data cables, spiralling up to the cheekbones. Her eyes glowed with the same blue-white as the Mark, but the light was rotten, more afterimage than luminescence. She walked hunched, feet barely clearing the floor, as if every step cost a piece of herself.

"Impostor," shadow-Ren sneered, tongue flicking over fangs that looked too sharp for her mouth. "You never belonged here, you know. Never finished anything."

Ren bared her own teeth—reflex, not show—and felt the new canines scrape her tongue, a tiny burst of blood that tasted like soldering iron and nostalgia. "That's not me," she said, "that's not us." She circled her twin, careful to keep a wall at her back. "You're just what happens if I let you win."

The double grinned. "You're what happens if you lose."

The entity—the Draft, the hunger at the heart of all this— was not just in the air. It was in her bones. Ren could feel it testing her, trying to slip a ghost of the Mark into every joint, every tendon, every line of memory she didn't keep on a tight leash. Her forearm burned, the scar now swirling with agitation, sending tendrils of light through her veins and up into her skull.

She risked a glance: Vincent was still on his knees, arms wrapped around himself, being mobbed by the chorus of his worst possible selves. There was a version in Crusader mail, voice like a locked door. There was a poet, pale and trembling, reciting his own eulogy in between stanzas. There was a monster, fangs red and eyes gold, crouched on Vincent's own back and hissing insults in his ear. The worst one, though, was the Vincent in the three-piece suit, who sat cross-legged on the dais and smirked, letting the others do the violence.

Ren moved to Vincent's side. The ground fought her, every step sticky, the void beneath wanting to pull her through to the next and the next and the next draft. Her own double stalked behind, the voice always at her back: "He'll turn on you. They always do. That's the story."

She put a hand on Vincent's shoulder. He flinched, almost lashed out, but her grip was iron—stronger than it should have been, stronger than she remembered from any human moment. She squeezed. "Hey. Look at me."

He didn't, so she yanked him, hard, and the poet and the monster and the soldier all fell away, leaving only the suit. The suit looked up at her, and for a second, it wore her own face—his old trick, mirroring whoever had the guts to oppose him.

"You're not those endings," she said, and this time she let the fangs show, half-smile and all. "You're the one who rewrote them. Remember?"

Vincent's real eyes, red-rimmed, locked on hers. "I'm terrified of what I am," he whispered.

She grinned wider. "Good. Means you're still you."

The scar on her arm flared, as if it was insulted, and the shadow-Ren shrieked, doubling over as if she'd been punched in the stomach. The world stuttered—every light flickered, every shadow snapped taut—then the illusions bled backwards into the stone, retreating in a slurp of unreality that left greasy after-images but nothing you could touch.

The cathedral shuddered, the walls buckling, arches bending like the bones of an animal in heat. The central dais, the altar at the heart of the void, broke open along a vertical seam, and the true face of the Draft Eternal surged out: not man, not woman, not even beast, but a writhing sheaf of parchment and fangs and hands that tore themselves apart and re-wove, forever, in real time. Its voice was every scream at once, layered with the feedback whine of a microphone too close to its own mortality.

*You. Will. Be. Edited.*

Ren's twin, now little more than a shuddering outline, lurched at her, claws out, aiming for the eyes. She caught the double's wrists and held them, feeling the strength of it, the raw, perfect rage of a version of herself who'd lost everything and only wanted company in the fall. The struggle was brief. Ren twisted, planted a foot, and snapped the double's arm at the elbow. It broke like dried wood, then re-knit itself, then broke again. She gripped harder, and this time she didn't let go. The scar sizzled, the double's skin bubbling up in angry blisters, then went dark, sloughing off like old latex paint. What was left was the original: her own face, human again, eyes dark and sad and apologetic.

"I didn't ask for this," the twin said.

Ren let go, and the shade folded in on itself, shrinking to a mote, then a dot, then nothing.

She staggered, wiped sweat and blood from her brow, and found Vincent standing upright, a little unsteady but no longer beset by his own ghosts. The monster at the dais was roaring, but its power was less. For the first time, the room sounded like it could be beat.

Mrs Barley was there too, moving with silent certainty, umbrella held at a perfect angle, feet spaced as if expecting the floor to vanish at any moment. She joined them without ceremony, her eyes alive with a cold, precise fury.

"It's weaker," Mrs Barley said, glancing at Ren's forearm. "You've changed the narrative. Keep doing it."

The entity, now exposed, coiled on itself, pages and limbs flapping, gnashing through every version of language it could remember. It lashed out with a tendril of liquid ink, catching Vincent across the chest. He grunted, staggered, but did not fall. Ren stepped between him and the monster, arms wide, and bared her fangs at the thing.

"You want to write the ending?" she shouted at it. "You'll have to come through me first."

The Draft tried, but every time it reached for her, the scar blazed and the attack rebounded, ricocheting into the walls and shattering chunks of the cathedral's logic. The illusions grew thinner; the monster's voice lost its perfect echo, became shriller, more panicked.

Vincent, not to be outdone, drew himself up and spat a mouthful of blood on the floor. "Go on then," he dared, eyes locked on the central heart of the thing. "Write it. I dare you."

Mrs Barley advanced with them, umbrella jabbing with every step, the fabric opening and closing with a click that sounded, in this place, like the guillotine of God.

Ren felt the scar on her arm sear, the skin blistering then healing in the same instant. She reached out, pressed her palm to the centre of the monster's mass, and pushed. The thing howled, the void buckled, and the cathedral began to collapse in on itself.

The trio tumbled as the world folded, the monster's form exploding into a storm of shredded paper and splinters. The air went white, then black, then silent.

Ren woke in a pile of rubble, Vincent at her side, Mrs Barley standing over them like a headstone. The void was gone, replaced by the cold and real stone of the old churchyard. Around them, the candles guttered, then winked out, one by one.

Zara's ghost hovered above, just long enough to say, "Well done, kid." Then she faded, a smile on her lips.

Ren looked at Vincent, who looked at Mrs Barley, who patted herself down and, finding no new disasters, actually let herself relax.

"Did we do it?" Ren asked.

Vincent grinned, showing teeth. "We rewrote the ending."

Mrs Barley nodded. "Let's go. It's almost dawn."

They walked out of the circle, Mark still bright but no longer burning. The world outside was raw, unfinished, but for the first time, it was theirs.

Somewhere, far beneath, the last echo of the Draft Eternal screamed its frustration. But even that faded with the coming day.

# TWENTY-ONE

The city was wrong.

They'd left the cemetery in what passed for morning—sun nowhere in evidence, sky the shade of wet newsprint, but definitely after dawn—and returned to find the world subtly off-axis. The streetlamps flickered with a grey-blue that should not have been possible without chemical help. Buildings leaned at new and suspicious angles, their brickwork writhing with a wet sheen as if everything was sweating through its foundations. The air itself was thick, not with fog, but with a density of narrative pressure that pressed on the ears and lungs like a migraine made meteorological.

Vincent caught the first whiff of it just past the end of the alley: iron, and the tell-tale odour of historical error. He stopped, dead centre of the pavement, and scanned for the source. It wasn't difficult. Across the way, the Houses of Parliament twisted, their silhouette rippling in the dawn like a melting print. The Thames was gone—just, gone—replaced by a

215

snaking vein of black ink that writhed and pulsed and spat up little clots of riverboat and police launch before swallowing them again.

Ren, at his elbow, let out a low whistle. "That's new," she said, voice pitched low, as if loudness might make it worse.

"Reality's still rebooting," Mrs Barley offered. She flicked her gaze along the horizon, lips pursed, as if compiling a shopping list of things that shouldn't exist. "Let's move."

The city was empty. Not a single human out, not even the night-shift detritus who usually haunted these blocks with kebab wrappers and football chants. Only the vampires, and the vampires' pets, and the ghosts of their future mistakes. As the trio approached the old Victoria Embankment, they found the coalition waiting: Germans, French, Trad and Mod, all clustered in uneasy truce along the banks of the non-existent river. Someone—probably Cass—had taped off the area with branded caution tape that read, in both English and French, "DO NOT CROSS: NARRATIVE IN PROGRESS."

Vincent found a spot atop a concrete stanchion, surveyed the assembly, and tried to ignore the itch at the base of his skull. It had been years since he'd felt a true premonition, but this one had the shape of a train coming and the sound of brakes already failed.

A ripple ran through the crowd as Mrs Barley climbed a traffic island and cleared her throat. "Quiet, please. We have limited time and, it seems, unlimited disaster." She nodded at the French and Germans, pleased they'd made it out more or less with the same numbers that went in. "We are facing an incursion of unprecedented scale. The Draft Eternal was not contained in the negative space. It is manifesting locally." She gestured at the city, as if the spasm in the skyline required further comment.

She flicked open the umbrella with a snap. "We will hold the line here. If we fail, London falls. If we succeed, we buy enough time for Miss Delacourt and her associates—" here, a nod to Zara's ghost, flickering in the periphery like a migraine aura, "—to finish the rewrite at the source."

Mrs Barley paused. She gave the crowd a look that, despite everything, was almost fond. "Let's get it over with."

Aurelia, front row with Cass and Nyx, raised a ring-lit phone and filmed the speech, mouthing "iconic" to her followers. Behind them, the French contingent adjusted sashes, checked their cuffs, and practised drawing their hidden blades in a way that was supposed to be inconspicuous but failed, spectacularly.

Vincent snorted, then stilled as the ground trembled underfoot. It started as a bass vibration—just the suggestion of motion—but in seconds, it became a true quake. The pavement split, fissures running like ink stains across the tarmac, and a roar built from below, not so much a sound as a verdict. The crowd staggered back as a patch of ground collapsed into the black, forming a ragged, pulsing mouth at the edge of the embankment.

From within, the army of the dead marched out.

It began with a trickle: a handful of revenants, crawling hand-over-knuckle up the slimy embankment like spiders on a plughole binge. Each one was different, and each the same. Their faces were stuck in the centuries that birthed them—some sporting ratty whiskers and rags, others in full Georgian regalia, complete with powdered wigs and the remnants of once-impressive mutton chops. Most wore the wounds of their last day: slashed throats, shattered skulls, holes where eyes had been swapped for pennies or just a lazy smear of rot.

Behind them came more: duellists, in once-fine coats, their jaws slack, sabres rusted to the colour of old wounds. Then the suffragette-bashers, fists studded with iron, faces blank with a kind of dogged chauvinism that could not be killed by logic or time. Next, the aristocrats: silk and velvet eaten by moths and history, but with teeth too big for their mouths, each set of incisors wired with extra rows for maximum predation. Some wore chains, dragging the links behind them like wedding veils. Others had crowns of thorns, or hats that pulsed with the dark energy of a thousand repressed scandals.

Vincent watched them crawl, shamble, then stride into formation on the embankment, and realised with a cold certainty that this was no mere zombie parade. These were the vampires erased from history: every one a revenant not just in body but in grievance, returned with a score to settle and a hunger sharpened by a century or more of nonexistence.

At their head marched Lord Ashcroft. His suit was midnight, the cut pure Savile Row, but it hung on him like a shroud. His skin—if it still counted as skin—was stretched so tight over his cheekbones that it gleamed under the streetlamps, and his mouth was set in a line that threatened, at any moment, to split into a new one and double his capacity for smug.

He raised a hand, and the army stopped, perfectly, in time.

Vincent watched as Ashcroft scanned the defenders, lingering with relish on every face. When he found Vincent, he saluted—an actual, two-fingered salute, as if they were old friends about to share a pint at the war's end.

"Did you think the Draft Eternal would come alone?" he called. His voice was a weapon: it travelled the length of the embankment, slicing through the air, freezing everyone in place. The revenant army echoed the line, a hundred dead mouths repeating it, some in perfect imitation, others stuttering or slurring, all of them hungry.

The coalition, to its credit, did not bolt. The Germans squared up, rifles at the ready, bayonets fixed with a sound like a million teeth grinding together. The French drew their blades, each one with a different flamboyant gesture, as if auditioning for a particularly murderous ballet. The Modernisers switched their phones to "Live" and began incantations, the screens strobing with the blue-white of in-progress magic. The Traditionalists, not to be outdone, began a low, guttural chant that set the air to trembling; even the dead paused at the resonance.

Vincent checked on Ren. She stood, feet planted, arms loose at her sides, eyes half-lidded in a way that signalled maximum readiness and minimum patience for bullshit. The scar on her forearm glowed, but not with the fever of old—now it was steady, disciplined, a tool rather than a curse. He caught her eye, and in the split second of contact, they exchanged more words than either had managed in a week.

*You good? / Only if you are. / Plan? / Don't die. / That's not a plan. / Works better than most.*

Ashcroft paced the line, his own generals behind him: a woman with a half-crushed face and a ceremonial truncheon, a child in sailor suit and sharpened fangs, a trio of twins in identical funeral gear, each clutching a copy of Debrett's. He stopped opposite Mrs Barley, and bowed.

"Mrs Barley," he said, "reduced to being a housekeeper,

these days? My, how the mighty have fallen. Or perhaps you've simply found your true station in life."

Mrs Barley, unflappable, returned the bow. "Lord Ashcroft. I see death has done little to improve your manners."

Ashcroft grinned, and the grin threatened to split his skull. "Manners are for the living. I am here for the finale, not the etiquette."

Vincent stepped forward, then, because someone had to. "If you're here to monologue, do us the favour of making it brief," he said. "Some of us have to live through this."

Ashcroft's eyes narrowed. "Still the cynic, Vincent. Still the coward."

He turned, raised his arms, and in perfect discipline, the army of the dead raised theirs, too.

"We will not be erased," he intoned. "We will not be footnotes in your miserable little stories. Tonight, we take the city back. Tonight, we show the world what it means to be the Draft Eternal."

The revenants howled, a noise not of any living thing but of every horror unvoiced in the British social contract.

Mrs Barley, voice as calm as ever, gave the counter-order. "Form ranks. On the signal, advance. Hold nothing back."

Vincent moved to Ren's side. "You know what to do," he said.

She nodded, cracked her neck, and smiled a thin, dangerous smile. "Yeah. Hit first. Ask questions after."

The crowd braced, all factions aligned: Germans with their guns, French with blades, Modernisers glowing with magic and anxiety, the Trads chanting at a volume that threatened the foundations of Whitehall. Mrs Barley raised her umbrella high, the tip sparking blue in the pre-dawn. Vincent and Ren crouched low, ready to spring.

On the far side, Ashcroft opened his arms, and the army of revenants moved as one.

Everything, for a moment, was perfectly still.

Then the world exploded.

The initial charge was less battle and more geological event.

A shockwave of revenants smashed into the front ranks of the coalition, bodies hitting with the inevitability of bad debt—impossible to dodge, impossible to ignore. The Germans, prepared for exactly this, let loose with their guns, cutting down the first rows. They dropped their rifles and picked up shields and bayonets, slicing downwards with a practised brutality that made the word "discipline" sound almost obscene. The undead tore at them with hands, jaws, and, occasionally, actual weaponry—rusted pistols, splintered lances, even the odd mortarboard swung as a bludgeon—but the line held. At least for the first ten seconds.

The French were another matter. Where the Germans met force with machine precision, the French met it with artistry: every sword stroke a calculated humiliation, every kill a spectacle. Marquis Deveraux led from the front, his sabre carving zigzags through the horde, his laughter audible even above the din. Each time a revenant went down, he paused to re-tie his cravat or dust off his sleeve, never missing a beat as he insulted both enemy and ally in three languages.

Vincent, shoulder to shoulder with Ren, punched through a knot of duellists, each one more desperate than the last. Their faces were warped by time and narrative, some barely human, others so perfectly preserved they seemed to have stepped straight out of a daguerreotype. The first he dispatched with a clean twist of the neck. The second, less obliging, bit through his wrist before Ren ripped its jaw free and spat it back at the mob, a gesture of pure, adolescent contempt.

"Thanks," Vincent muttered, shaking the hand to speed the healing.

Ren grinned, blood streaked up one cheek. "You owe me a drink."

He would have replied, but a suffragette-basher swung a truncheon into his ribs, crumpling the shirt and the bones underneath. Vincent howled, caught the man by the lapels, and drove his fangs into the meat of his neck, letting the hunger ride him just long enough to hollow the revenant from the inside out.

They fought as a pair, a dance choreographed by necessity and instinct. Where Vincent went low, Ren went high; where Ren over-committed, Vincent covered her flank. She was faster —infinitely so—her new nature amplifying every reflex until she left afterimages in her own wake. But she was reckless, raw, the scar on her arm flaring with every kill, the blue-white spiralling up her veins like a second, more dangerous pulse.

He watched her for signs of losing control. The first came within a minute: she downed a revenant, then kept biting, kept tearing, even after the body went limp. Vincent yanked her up by the collar, snarling, "Not them. Not yet."

She blinked, shook off the haze, and threw herself back into the melee, but the edge in her smile was wild, almost joyous.

Everywhere, the world was ending.

The Modernisers, clustered at mid-field, wielded their phones and ring lights like wands. Each enchantment was tailored for maximum spectacle: Instagram filters that burned the eyes from revenants' sockets, TikTok memes that looped until the undead collapsed from pure narrative exhaustion, a Snapchat curse that forced every attacking corpse to dance the Macarena for ninety seconds before being allowed to rejoin the fray. Cass, at the centre of it, live-streamed the whole mess, his narration switching from English to German to Mandarin with the frequency of a nervous tic.

But the revenants learned. They started tearing down the ring lights, bashing the Modernisers with their own hardware, countering every spell with a makeshift weapon or a counter-narrative of their own. Several times, Vincent saw a Moderniser drop their phone, only for a revenant to pick it up and use it as a bludgeon, the irony almost enough to make him laugh even as he ducked a swipe at his head.

The Trads stood in a circle, arms linked, their chant so deep it warped the air around them. The sound made Vincent's skull itch, set his teeth on edge, but it worked: every revenant that passed through the perimeter slowed, then staggered, then burst in a spray of cold, blue fire. At the circle's centre, Mrs Barley barked orders and corrections, her umbrella flashing in time with the chant, the tip now glowing a shade of blue so bright it left spots on Vincent's vision.

The Germans, disciplined as ever, were not immune to loss. Within the first two minutes, two vampires went down, torn apart by a group of skeletonised duellists whose pistols spat not bullets but bone fragments, each one burning with the same black ink as the river. The casualties were hoisted up and paraded by the revenants, who used the bodies as banners, waving them with the mockery of schoolboys at a rival's funeral.

The French fared better, but not by much. Marquis Deveraux took a cane-sword to the shoulder, the blade sliding in and out like a harpoon. He staggered, snarled, then snapped the sword in half and drove both ends through the eyes of his attacker, taking three more down in the process. The blood—his and theirs—flew in elegant arcs, spattering the floor in what might have been calligraphy if anyone had time to appreciate it.

Vincent and Ren made for the centre, fighting towards the source of the mess. Every step was a battle: the ground itself writhed, hands reached up from the cracks to grab at their ankles, the air thick with particles of dust and blood and the shredded remnants of every bad idea ever committed to the London record.

Nyx, working the back line, thumped out a bass rhythm on a pair of enchanted speakers. Each drop sent a shockwave through the revenant ranks, buckling their knees, shattering their teeth, sometimes knocking the heads clean off. But the horde was endless. After three drops, the speakers began to spark and whine, the wards inside breaking under the pressure of so many counter-voices. Nyx's face, always pale, now looked translucent, veins darkening in time with the music.

Vincent saw the moment it happened: a revenant, dressed as a Victorian constable, lobbed a severed hand at Nyx. The hand landed on the speaker, shorting the wires and sending a backflow of raw energy into Nyx's chest. He collapsed, twitching, as the wall of revenants surged forward, trampled the DJ, and kept coming.

Zara's ghost, trailing the edge of the fight, blinked in and out of visibility. Each time she materialised, she flared with a cold, ultraviolet brilliance, a miniature aurora that stunned the undead long enough for someone else to take the kill. But every appearance left her dimmer, thinner. By the third, she was barely a silhouette, her features drifting apart at the edges.

"Don't stop!" she called, her voice a Doppler effect that travelled slower than her own movement. "The Draft is watching! The more you fight, the more it tries to rewrite—"

Her words were cut by a volley of bone bullets, which passed straight through her but clipped three Modernisers in the face. Cass, in the scrum, caught sight of her and yelled, "You're glitching! Hold the frequency!"

Zara flickered, managed a ragged laugh, and said, "That's what I do best."

On the far side of the field of battle, Lord Ashcroft strolled through the carnage with unhurried grace, his lieutenants forming a cordon of absolute violence around him. He never lifted a finger, never dirtied his hands, but everywhere he went, the battle tipped in his favour: the dead rose faster, the undead faltered, the odds rebalanced. He stopped at the front line, inspected the French like a drill sergeant, and plucked a blade from the hand of a dying revenant.

He twirled the sword, smiled, and pointed it at Deveraux. "*En garde,* Marquis."

Deveraux, half-delirious with blood loss and glee, bowed deeply. "*Après vous,* milord."

They clashed, blades hissing and shrieking, the fight so fast even Vincent struggled to follow it. Ashcroft's style was pure theatre—every riposte a backhanded insult, every parry a pointed reminder of superiority. Deveraux, for all his flair, was losing. The swordplay grew tighter, the circles smaller, until Ashcroft flicked the sabre from Deveraux's hand, caught it mid-air, and rammed both blades through the Marquis's ribcage.

Deveraux gasped, blood spraying in a perfect parabola, and managed, *"Touché."*

Ashcroft withdrew the blades, wiped them on Deveraux's own sash, and tossed them aside. He did not look at the body as it slid to the ground, but instead turned his attention to the next row of defenders, eyes bright with anticipation.

# TWENTY-TWO

Ren, seeing the loss, bared her fangs and charged. Vincent followed, because letting her go alone was suicide, and because she would never let him hear the end of it if he hung back.

They met Ashcroft's vanguard head-on. The twins in funeral garb lunged as one; Vincent caught the first by the wrist, twisted, and drove the bone through the second's eye socket.

Ren tackled the truncheon woman, snapping her spine with a bear hug and then tossing the body into the crowd behind, where it vanished in a scrum of snapping teeth and hungry fingers.

Vincent paused to watch. It was beautiful. Monstrous, but beautiful.

Vincent wondered, in the back of his mind, if this was what Carmine had meant all those years ago, on the roof in Florence: "You'll never be more alive than when you're past death." At the time, he'd thought it was a chat-up line. Now, watching Ren punch a hole through three revenants and land a double-kick on the jaw of a fourth, he got it.

The pair of them worked through the horde with all the elegance of a bin lorry in a rainstorm. Gone was the reluctant coordination; now there was only a kind of chemical synchronicity, a relay of killing so fluid they barely had to look to know where the other would be. Vincent swept the left. Ren swept the right. Every so often, they'd trade off, one ducking to let the other leap, one punching through so the other could finish. It was partnership, at the level of the gene.

The wall of revenants surged, pressed by the coalition's last-ditch formation, but for every one that dropped to a bayonet or burning ring-light, two more slithered from the cracks. The ground bucked beneath Vincent's boots, splitting in a fault-line that ran straight to the Thames and, presumably, the bottom of the story.

He caught Ren's sleeve. "That's not the main event," he said. "It's just warming up."

She wiped blood from her cheek, the scar on her arm pulsing with a cold, vindictive light. "You think?"

He pointed. The black ink that had replaced the Thames was climbing, spider-like, up the embankment, pooling in eddies before sluicing into a storm drain marked with the crown and an indecipherable sigil. The fluid was impossibly viscous, moving as though it had a job to do and a strict deadline.

Vincent felt the pull, like gravity but more personal. It dragged at the roots of his spine, at the softest bits of his brain—the bits that kept the nightmares behind a polite velvet rope. He gritted his teeth, muttered "Showtime," and followed the current.

Ren didn't hesitate. Mrs Barley, despite a faceful of narrative shrapnel and a left arm now bent at a non-regulation angle, matched their pace. "Don't get separated," she intoned, as if the only thing worse than death was having to file separate incident reports.

The tunnel under the embankment was not a tunnel, but a throat: lined in yellowed parchment and veined with old ink, puckered every few yards by the faces of failed legislation and dead vampire ordinances. They passed a rib of Queen Anne's signatures, a weeping abscess of Victorian séance transcripts, a mass grave of council meeting minutes that had never reached quorum. The air thickened with the scent of scorched vellum and the dark, sweet bite of printer's toner.

At the heart of the chamber, the Draft Eternal waited.

The throne was the size of a small mausoleum, constructed from stacks of manuscript paper, all of it slightly singed at the edges, every sheet tattooed with redlines and margin notes and angry, looping corrections in a dozen different hands. It sat atop a dais of crushed bone, the marrow hollowed and repurposed as channels for the ink that pumped

It sat atop a dais of crushed bone, the marrow hollowed and repurposed as channels for the ink that pumped through the cavern's veins. The ink glistened in black arterial rivers, sluicing from the base of the throne and pooling in viscous deltas at the foot of the steps, where it shimmered and gurgled as if eager for use. The throne itself was an architectural insult to the concept of permanence: a fortress of stacked manuscript, its flanks bolstered with armrests of jawbone and scapula, vertebral columns lashed together as bannisters, and every available surface papered with loose leaves annotated in red, blue, or the sort of iridescent green that only appears in nightmares and government stationery.

The seat was occupied, of course.

The Draft Eternal unfurled from the chair in increments, refusing to commit to a single outline. At first glance, it might have been a man—draped in the robes of a judge, perhaps, or a council Speaker; but every second revealed more: the robe was nothing but layered manuscript, stitched with sinews of blotted ribbon, alive with the twitch and rustle of uncountable pages in agitation. Where a face should be, dozens instead, each half-glimpsed before it dissolved or was torn away: a child's mouth screaming through a pensioner's eyes; a wolfish snout melting into the slurred lips of a drunken poet; an aristocrat's jawline, already chewed through by the next revolution. The heads rotated, flickered, sometimes split, always replaced.

It had arms—many, most of the time—but never a fixed number. Some were the quilled hands of an old scribe, others were gnarled and veined like roots, some wore white silk gloves, but all of them clutched or gestured or pointed, always as if making a final, inarguable motion. One hand gripped a gavel the size of a human thigh, another clutched a massive sheaf of papers so over-edited the edges smoked where the ink ran. Some hands wrote continuously, bleeding text onto the air itself, where words hung for a moment before they too were erased.

It watched Vincent's approach with a patience made obscene by scale.

The honour guard of revenants parted. No two alike, but all recognisably failures—forgotten vampires in threadbare court dress, police uniforms, medieval executioner hoods, or the haphazard tatters of the recently erased. Their faces were a study in damage and disappointment: some chewed their own lips to ribbons, others smiled in a way that could only be explained as an anatomical error, others still just goggled in silent terror at the floor. They bowed, or tried to, but most just jerked in synchrony as if yanked by a single string.

At the head of this parade stood Lord Ashcroft. His once-pristine suit was a palimpsest of stains and tears, but he wore it as if still the best-dressed man in Westminster. Blood streaked one glove, a monocle hung by a literal thread, and his hair (never a point of pride) now blazed in white streaks where the Draft Eternal's aura had burned it clean. He beamed at Vincent with the confidence of a man who has lost everything but the ability to lose face.

"Mr Lupo," he called, as if welcoming an old tennis partner to Centre Court. "You're just in time. The Draft's been awaiting your redline." He pivoted, with the grandiloquence of a Shakespearean ghost, to present Vincent to the throne. "Shall I announce you, or do you wish to introduce yourself?"

Vincent bared his fangs, a deliberate show. His feet squelched on the paper-scummed floor as he advanced, each step slower than the last, the weight of all the eyes (and at least two mouths) of the Draft Eternal dragging at him. He knew, in some perfunctory nerve, that turning and fleeing would be the only honest instinct left, but the rest of him was too bloody-minded to oblige.

Behind him, Ren matched his pace. She limped a little, the scar still smoking on her arm where it had burned through one of her tattoos. Her new eyes, red but clear, swept the throne room with undisguised loathing. Next to her, Mrs Barley stumped along, umbrella clacking as she tested the terrain for hidden traps.

The silence gathered, not by accident but by intention.

A hundred faces on the Draft Eternal shifted towards Vincent. Its voice was neither loud nor soft but absolute, bypassing the ears and vibrating directly in the sinuses and teeth.

"VINCENT LUPO," it intoned, every syllable overlapping with a dozen edits, so the name arrived both as a chant and as a sneer. "YOU ARE THE AGGREGATE OF ALL YOUR ERRORS. YOU ARE EVERY VERSION OF YOURSELF THAT HAS EVER FAILED TO FINISH, EVERY DRAFT THAT HAS EVER BEEN ABANDONED, EVERY LINE THAT HAS DIED BETWEEN THE FIRST WORD AND THE FINAL DOT." The faces flickered: wolf, man, woman, child, then all at once. "YOU WERE ALWAYS OURS."

Ren, not in the mood for monologue, spat on the dais, the phlegm burning a hole in the top layer of manuscript.

The entity's faces looked at her, then back to Vincent.

Ashcroft cleared his throat. "I believe the Draft wishes you to kneel," he said. "Symbolic gesture, et cetera. You know how these things go."

Vincent did not kneel. Instead, he spoke, and his voice was hoarse, but steady: "If I'm your draft, then let's get the red pen out."

A ripple went through the court: the revenants shuddered, every pair of eyes widening, a few collapsing outright. Ashcroft's smile wavered, and for a brief, delicious moment, he looked as if he regretted ever volunteering to be the mouthpiece for the End of Days.

The Draft Eternal's hands flurried in anger, and the throne shivered, a cascade of paper snowing off its flanks. "YOU CANNOT EDIT WHAT YOU ARE," it hissed, this time in the thin, reedy voice of a child at bedtime. "THE STORY ENDS AS IT BEGINS: WITH BLOOD. YOUR BLOOD."

Mrs Barley, at Vincent's elbow, murmured, "Banal, isn't it?" She handed Ren a sharpened pencil. "You might need this."

Vincent squared his shoulders, fangs fully out now, his every nerve ending singing with terror and an equally perverse joy. He eyed Ashcroft, who looked for once unsure, then addressed the throne.

"You've rewritten everyone else," Vincent said. "But you never made it stick. What makes you think I'll go quietly?"

The throne's faces grinned as one.

Ashcroft, recapturing his role, spread his arms. "Oh, but you've never faced a proper edit, old boy. The little errors that build up. Eventually, you forget you ever wrote yourself any other way."

The room darkened as the entity gathered itself, more pages and faces pouring from its back, arms multiplying, every one of them gunning for Vincent's soul. The voices overlapped now, every contradiction, every regret, every cowardice he'd ever owned or borrowed.

The next step belonged to Vincent, or to whatever version of him survived this next round.

He drew in a breath thick with the scent of old paper and new death. "Ren?" he said.

She flexed her claws, not looking away from the horror on the throne. "Ready."

He looked to Mrs Barley, who nodded, umbrella poised at a bureaucratic 45 degrees.

Then he stepped forward, and the world narrowed to the length of the shadow cast by the throne.

The Draft Eternal leaned in, faces warping into a single mass of mouths and teeth.

Vincent bared his fangs, and smiled. "I'll take it from here."

The chamber erupted in screaming, ink, and movement.

The entity surged.

A hundred hands, a thousand claws, the piranha snap of gnashing mouths: all of it met Vincent at full speed, and for a heartbeat he felt the old panic, the buried urge to run and keep running until the world had looped back on itself and erased him for good. But then Ren screamed, not in fear but in blood-howl, and he remembered who he was.

Vincent launched himself at the throne, fangs bared, and fingers crooked to claws, striking a chord of pure, destructive glee. The Draft Eternal's nearest limb—a sweep of manuscript pages, laced with barbed wire and crowned with a fist made of stapled skulls—met him with a backhand blow. It should have thrown him to the opposite wall, but Vincent caught the arm in both hands and bit down, shredding through the manuscript in a gout of black ink and raw, burning pain. The ink sprayed, hissing, onto his tongue; it tasted of printer's toner, acid, and the last ten things he'd ever regretted saying.

He spat it out, kicked off the arm, and slashed his claws

through the next wave of faces. Each face screamed, then split, then fused into new, uglier iterations: a schoolteacher's mask with a gavel for a tongue; an infant's head set on a ring of rotating dentures; his own face, laughing at him with the mirthless pleasure of a man watching his own funeral from the audience.

Ren was beside him, a blur of blood and hoodie, her fists driving straight through the monster's torso and coming out the far side trailing blue-white fire. She roared, grabbed a handful of the entity's own paper innards, and tore, leaving a cavity that gushed narrative fragments and the sour smell of old toner. Where her hands ripped, the ink caught fire and burned, the flames running in reverse up her arms but failing to touch her skin.

"That all you've got?" she snarled, voice cracking with the force of it.

The Draft Eternal shrieked back, its voices warbling through a dozen languages, some of them not even invented yet. "WE ARE INFINITE DRAFTS. WE ARE THE EDIT THAT UNMAKES YOU."

It struck with a bundle of hooked quills, aiming straight for her throat. Ren ducked, then drove a knee into the base of the throne, shattering vertebrae and making the whole seat shudder. Vincent saw his moment, dived under the distraction, and scrambled up the paper-strewn steps, tearing handholds wherever the entity's flesh got in his way. Each time he dug in, the wound closed, but not before leaving a trail of blackened ash in its wake.

At the edge of the dais, Mrs Barley faced down the revenant honour guard. She raised her umbrella, now open and alive with a lattice of glowing sigils—letters and punctuation marks strobing in sequence, like a data packet mid-teleport. With a brisk snap of the wrist, she jabbed the umbrella's tip into the ground. The glow flared, then pulsed outward in a circle. The nearest revenants, caught in the light, froze as if someone had hit the pause button on their narrative. Their feet sank into the floor, ink rose up to their waists, and their voices stuttered to a helpless staccato.

She followed up with a phrase that sounded like three contracts and a libel suit colliding: "On authority of the Court of Pale Affairs, London Chapter, by the clause of Exigent Continuance, I deny you standing."

The ring of sigils snapped tight, pinning half the army where they stood.

Lord Ashcroft, less affected by the ritual, tried to step over a trapped footman. The footman grabbed his ankle and yanked, sending Ashcroft sprawling onto his knees. He still managed to look dignified, even as his face slid through five different expressions of outrage.

On the throne, the Draft Eternal fought to expel Vincent. The entity writhed, every limb and face squirming to unseat him, but Vincent clung on, biting and tearing and letting the old rage—against history, against himself—do most of the driving.

He found a mouth, bigger than the rest, and shoved his hand in up to the wrist. The mouth bit down, chewing through muscle and sinew, but he forced his other hand in too, prying the jaws apart with a snap that sent a spray of teeth and script into the air.

"YOU ARE THE MISTAKE," the mouth wailed. "YOU ARE THE DRAFT THAT SHOULD HAVE DIED."

Vincent laughed, because there was nothing else for it. "Then you should've had better editors."

He pulled himself higher, where the faces thinned, and found what might have been the original: a blank page, perfectly white, embedded at the crown of the throne like a hidden heart. It radiated a cold, hungry pressure—every word he'd never written, every possibility never realised. It hated him.

Ren, not to be outdone, scaled the flank of the throne in three leaps. She caught a tentacle of bound parchment around her waist and used it to swing up beside Vincent, grabbing a fistful of his ruined shirt for balance.

"You got it?" she barked.

"Working on it," he spat, black ink streaming from the corner of his mouth.

Ren nodded, braced her feet, and punched straight through the next wave of faces. It was pure animal power—no technique, no finesse, just the refusal to be eaten by any narrative, even her own.

Together they reached for the blank page.

At the base, Mrs Barley redirected her efforts, umbrella now closed but held like a rapier. She advanced through the immobilised ranks, reciting ritual phrases at every step. "Nullify," she said, and a group of Trad revenants blinked out of existence. "Void," and the next set of faces melted into grey sludge. When one Moderniser broke free and lunged, she swatted him with the umbrella, leaving a barcode-shaped scar across his face.

"Would it kill you to help?" she shouted up at Vincent and Ren.

"Almost certainly," Vincent replied, but reached down and offered her a bloody hand anyway.

Mrs Barley eyed the hand, then climbed, muttering under her breath about unsafe workplace conditions. She reached the throne just as Vincent and Ren managed to expose the core.

The entity recoiled, but the wounds they'd inflicted would not heal. Instead, it tried to fold in on itself, to create a recursive knot of stories within stories, a suffocating infinity that would choke them out before they reached the centre.

Vincent, Ren and Mrs Barley all reached for the page. It fought like a living thing—slippery, cold, venomous—but together they clamped down and pulled.

The scream that resulted was not of this world.

It blew the top off the cavern, sent a storm of shredded manuscript through the air, and made every revenant in the chamber seize up like a bad case of tetanus. Even Ashcroft, still skulking at the periphery, doubled over, his gloved hand flying to his heart.

Ren howled right back, her voice a match for the entity's. Vincent thought his eardrums might actually turn inside out, but he didn't stop pulling.

Then the page tore.

Not all the way. Not yet. But a hairline split ran down the centre, leaking ink that glowed blue-white and sizzled on contact with the air. The monster reeled, clawed at its own head, and for a glorious moment, Vincent saw every one of its faces gaping in pure, unadulterated terror.

Above them, Zara's ghost steadied herself.

She hovered, half-disintegrated, hands clasped at her chest as if bracing for the pain to come. For a second, she met Vincent's gaze, and he saw what she was about to do.

"Don't you dare," he said, but it was too late.

Zara dived.

Her ghost-light flared, pure and blinding, burning through the darkness with a brightness so absolute it turned the ink clouds to nothing, erased the rain of pages, and left a negative afterimage on every surface. She plummeted through the monster's body, leaving a wake of fire, and hit the anchoring runes at the core with a force that collapsed the space around it.

Her scream was not a scream but a word: NO.

The runes buckled, warped, then burst. All at once, every page in the room caught fire. The monster howled, its voices diverging into chaos, each mouth shrieking a different dialect of despair. The faces peeled off, dissolved, then spat out fresh ones in a last-ditch effort to defend itself.

The whole throne buckled, then detonated in a geyser of ink and blank paper. Vincent, Ren, and Mrs Barley tumbled off the dais, bouncing down the steps and into the shallow pool of ink below, where it hissed but no longer burned.

Above them, the entity shrieked, its form dissolving in waves. The honour guard, suddenly free, howled and fled into the shadows. Lord Ashcroft, now missing half his face and a good deal of dignity, crawled away on hands and knees, leaving a trail of black smears.

The Draft Eternal fought to reform, but every page they'd torn away refused to rejoin the mass. Instead, the pieces floated in the air, circling the throne room in a slow, lazy orbit, each one inscribed with a single word: END.

Mrs Barley coughed, spat out a mouthful of blue-white ink, and got to her feet. She looked at the ruined umbrella, shrugged, and threw it at the dissolving entity. The umbrella landed perfectly upright, the tip skewering the last face as it screamed itself out of existence.

Vincent lay back in the ink, exhausted. Ren landed beside him, equally spent but grinning, blood and ink in equal measure across her face.

"Not bad," she said, staring up at the storm of dissolving pages.

He coughed, then laughed. "I'll take a blank ending over a bad one any day."

"So that's it?" Ren asked. "We win?"

Mrs Barley considered this, then said. "We win."

# TWENTY-THREE

The surviving coalition staggered out of the carnage in ones and two, the casualties outnumbering the living, but the living more defiant for it. Even the Germans—never a people to emote, especially not in the presence of French witnesses—looked a bit shell-shocked. Their uniforms were tattered, medals lost in the scrum, faces streaked with a substance no one would ever admit to being actual tears. The French, though less numerically intact, had rallied around their fallen leader, Deveraux, whom they carried out on a crude stretcher cannibalised from a revenant bones. Nobody mentioned the absurdity; nothing was more French than to suffer in style.

The Modernisers were worse off, most of them reduced to a jittering rabble. Aurelia had gone full influencer, live-streaming herself dabbing ink-blood from her eyelids, which she insisted on referring to as "aesthetic battle residue."

Vincent and Ren stood at the epicentre, locked in a moment

of post-traumatic standoff. Feral was not so much a state as a dimension, and right now they occupied it to the exclusion of any human logic. Vincent's teeth were still out, and not just out but full display, canine tips beaded with the last shreds of ink-blood. His eyes—always a reliable shade of cynic's brown—now burned crimson, pulsing with aftershocks of violence and a hunger that had nothing to do with metaphysics.

His limbs shook. At first it was only the hands, but then the tremor ran up his arms, through his chest, and into the tight bundle of nerves at the base of his skull. It took everything to hold it back: the urge to pounce, to keep shredding until every possibility in the world was tamed, bled dry, and filed under "done." He locked his knees and tried to focus on something other than the rhythm of Ren's pulse, or the weird blue fire still running under her skin.

He failed.

A noise—barely a noise, just the scrape of movement—made him lurch sideways, claws snapping out. He nearly tore off his own sleeve in the process.

Ren was faster. She caught his elbow, grip vice-tight, and steadied him with a force that seemed completely at odds with her skeletal, hoodie-and-jeans profile. She didn't flinch. Didn't even blink. Her new eyes—scarlet now, not the eager brown she'd had in life—held his with a clarity that felt both predatory and, disturbingly, maternal.

"Still in there, Lupo?" she asked, voice low but steady.

He managed to nod, and forced the teeth back behind his lips. "More or less. The less is doing most of the heavy lifting, though."

She grinned, and the fangs showed. "Let it. You've earned a minute."

He tried to laugh, but it came out as a wet bark. "Not sure the world can afford me unfiltered."

Ren squeezed his arm. "World's on its own now. Our bit's done." She flicked a glance at the rest of the coalition, then back at Vincent. "You good?"

He considered the question, then decided to answer honestly, for once. "No. But I'm better."

A shadow passed overhead—literal this time—and for a second Vincent tensed, expecting a re-manifestation, a final, vengeful swipe from the Draft. But it was just Mrs Barley, umbrella now missing its tip and half its handle, but still wielded with the authority of someone who was ready for whatever the universe might throw at her next.

She looked like hell. Her neat hair was singed at the ends, blouse torn at the collar, one shoe missing and the other replaced with what appeared to be a Moderniser's discarded Croc. Yet her poise was untouched; she picked her way through the debris as if it were a slightly messy town hall meeting rather than a post-apocalyptic abattoir.

Mrs Barley surveyed the survivors with a look that managed to be both clinical and vaguely patronising. She noted the casualty ratio, the unclaimed bits of shrapnel, the way the French had already formed a grievance committee. She paused at Vincent and Ren, clocked the way their hands were still joined, and arched an eyebrow in what could have passed for mild approval.

"Time, Mr Lupo?" she asked, voice even.

He squinted at the pale smudge of wrist where a watch had once been. "Little after three, I think. Not that I trust this place for accuracy."

Mrs Barley nodded, as if this was a satisfactory answer to a question she hadn't actually asked. She pulled her battered clipboard from under one arm, flipped to a fresh page, and began to write.

Ren peered over. "What's the report say?"

Mrs Barley didn't look up. "It says 'Resolution achieved. With amendments.'"

She finished the line, then snapped the notebook shut with a click that echoed in the new silence. "Well done, all. Now, please: let's not stand around congratulating ourselves. The clean-up will be ghastly, and I for one would like a head start."

For a second, no one moved. Then the survivors—French, German, Modern, Trad—began to pick themselves up, some in twos, some dragging the less fortunate, some just following out of pure, tribal inertia.

Vincent glanced at Ren, and she at him. There was no need for words.

They followed Mrs Barley towards the remains of the archway, through the static snow of burning paper and the last, lonely puffs of blue-white ash. Somewhere behind them, the Draft's final pages fluttered in the wind, curling in on themselves until they became indistinguishable from the shadows.

At the threshold, Vincent turned for one last look. The cavern was smaller than it had been—shrunk, maybe, by the absence of narrative, or just by the loss of anything left to prove. He saw the empty dais, the pooling ink, the scattered bones of a hundred years of unfinished stories. He saw, for a flicker, the ghost of Zara Delacourt—now little more than a ripple of light at the edge of vision. She wasn't smiling, but she wasn't scowling, either.

He raised a hand, unsure if she'd see, then remembered: she'd always been better at endings than he was.

Ren nudged him. "Come on. Before Mrs Barley leaves us on the wrong side of history."

He nodded, let the animal recede, and stepped out into the new world.

The world outside was waiting, as worlds always did: indifferent to the horrors recently banished from its underbelly, keen to resume the more familiar torments of cold rain, financial malaise, and the uniquely English anxiety of missed bin collections. The survivors emerged from the crumbling archway in a staggered column, Mrs Barley at the fore, Ren and Vincent close behind, and the rest—those few who had not been erased or combusted or shuffled into the margins—straggling after.

The archway, once the ceremonial entrance to the Parliament's oldest sub-basement, now shimmered with the afterglow of magical overuse. As the last foot passed its threshold, the stones sealed behind them with a damp, reluctant thud, like the final pages of an overlong book. None of the humans on the street—if there were any left, at this hour—so much as looked up. The only sound was the Doppler rise and fall of sirens, distant but insistent, as if the city was already rehearsing its next tragedy.

The first to reassemble were the Germans. There were only seven of them now, but they formed up with the rigidity of a parade ground. Their uniforms—now mostly rags—were re-buttoned and tucked as best as possible, and every surviving officer saluted Falkenhayn with a precision that belied the open wounds on half their faces. Falkenhayn himself stood at parade rest, a rag tied over one eye, the other fixed dead ahead.

The French were less formal, but no less dignified. The survivors formed a line and bowed deeply—first to Mrs Barley, then to Vincent and Ren and finally to the Germans.

Aurelia and her Modernisers were still at the rear, sifting the night for anything salvageable: a working phone, a discarded vape, a functional ring light. Aurelia herself, battered but ever glamorous, dabbed her lips, then snapped a final selfie in front of the Parliament's cracked door. Vincent had to admire the commitment to narrative.

For a long moment, nothing happened. No words, just the cold snap of winter air and the slowly dissipating scent of burning manuscript. The survivors stood there, all of them, blinking at a world that had somehow failed to notice its own brush with unmaking.

Then, slowly, the Germans and French began to peel away, each group moving as if called by an inaudible bugle.

When they were gone, Mrs Barley finally exhaled. The effect was less relief, more the completion of a checklist item.

She glanced at Ren, who was watching the French with a kind of scientific awe.

"You're in control?" Mrs Barley asked, pointedly.

Ren flexed her fingers, testing the claws. "If I wasn't, you'd be missing a face."

Mrs Barley nodded, then, with less ceremony than a Post-it note, asked Vincent the same.

He took a breath. "Let's just say I could really do with a drink."

The words hung in the air, a benediction and a warning.

Above them, the ghost of Zara Delacourt lingered in the sodium-orange glow of a streetlamp. She was little more than a shimmer, now, a negative of herself, but it followed them a few paces, then paused at the edge of the light.

Vincent looked back. His jaw set, the grief deeper now that there was room for it.

Ren stepped up, close but not touching. Her voice was so quiet only he could hear. "She'd tell us not to waste it."

He didn't trust himself to reply, so he just nodded, once.

Mrs Barley was already several paces ahead, briskly shepherding the Modernisers towards the nearest safe house. The rest would disperse, as they always did—into history, into myth, into the next failed revolution.

Vincent stood in the chill for a while, watching the city rebuild its fiction of normalcy. He felt Ren beside him, could hear the thump of her heart, now tuned to the same strange frequency as his own.

Eventually, she spoke again. "Humanity's safe. For now. Pity about us."

He snorted. "Not the first time, won't be the last."

Ren grinned, all teeth. "Then we write the next chapter ourselves."

Vincent took her hand, a little surprised when she let him. They walked down the empty street, the dawn not quite ready to start, but the night no longer holding them hostage.

Behind them, the last spark of Zara's ghost drifted up, circled once above their heads, and winked out with the softest possible pop.

The world, for once, seemed finished with its story.

**THE END**

# NOTE FROM THE AUTHOR

Hi,

Thanks so much for reading *Rewrite the Dead*!

It was a lot of fun to write. I truly hope it was an entertaining read.

If you enjoyed the book, I would be incredibly grateful if you'd be so kind as to leave a review.

Reviews really help authors for a number of reasons, not least, providing feedback on what readers like and improving visibility of the book on online retail sites.

Thanks in advance and I look forward to reading your thoughts.

Jon

# ABOUT THE AUTHOR

Jon Smith is the bestselling author of more than 50 books for children, teens, and adults. His books have sold over half a million copies and have been published in seven languages.

In addition to writing books, Jon is an award-winning screenwriter and musical theatre lyricist and librettist with productions at the Birmingham Hippodrome, Belfast Waterfront, London's Park Theatre and PJPAC, Kuala Lumpur.

A father of four, he lives near Liverpool with his wife and their two school-age children.

When he grows up he'd like to be a librarian.

www.jonsmith.net

X x.com/jonsmith_author

instagram.com/jonsmith_author

goodreads.com/jonsmith_author

amazon.com/author/jonsmith

facebook.com/authorjonsmith

# MAILING LIST

Want to receive advance information about future publications?

Fancy exclusive access to freebies, special offers and bonus material?

Feel that your life isn't complete without Jon's monthly musings about writing, reading and publishing?

There's a solution! Sign up today to Jon's mailing list:

**https://jonsmith.net/mailing-list**

# THE FANG & LOATHING TRILOGY

BAL
KON
media